Beauty and the Beast

"The perfect love!"
USA Today

"Humanity and emotion that shine
like a beacon—
an elegant, sophisticated love story
the likes of which
television has never seen"
Hollywood Reporter

"Old-fashioned, shamelessly lyrical
romanticism"
The New York Times

"A fantasy for everyone to love . . .
TV's most imaginative,
romantic and decent-hearted show!"
People

Beauty and the Beast

A Novel by
BARBARA HAMBLY

based on the series created by
RON KOSLOW

AVON BOOKS ◆ NEW YORK

AVON BOOKS
A division of
The Hearst Corporation
105 Madison Avenue
New York, New York 10016

First Avon Books Printing: October 1989

Special thanks to
Ann, Anne, Nancy, Robin, and Mimi
for assistance, information,
and expertise

To the people without whom
I wouldn't know enough about love
to write about it:
My Parents

Beauty and the Beast

One

LOOKING back on the night of April 12, Catherine knew there had to have been something she could have done. Some way she could have gotten out of this, some action she could have taken—or not taken—to avoid the whole situation, though she wasn't quite sure what. That was the worst of it.

At least, she thought that was the worst of it until the bandages came off her eyes.

She had a long time—endless time—of lying in darkness, and terror, and throbbing pain, to think about that before anyone came, and much of that time she spent trying to pinpoint just where she could have hopped off that particular Slow Local to Hell.

Her father's offices—and after two years with Chandler and Prasker, Catherine still hadn't come to think of them as *her* offices—were on West 57th Street around the corner from Central Park South, and his office, if not hers, commanded a respectable view of the Avenue of the Americas, something not to be sneered at on a lovely April day like this one. Her own, as befitted a junior

1

member of the firm, even if she *was* Charles Chandler's daughter, was an interior room, and maybe that fact had something to do with how little time she managed to spend there. All the rosewood paneling and designer sculpture in the world didn't alter the fact that there was no window. She didn't know how the other junior lawyers stood it.

That particular Monday she showed up late—late enough that her breezy "'Morning . . .'" drew a teasing "Not anymore, it's not" from the receptionist as she passed the front desk, slipping off her overcoat and trying to pretend she'd been there for at least an hour.

"Picky, picky," she tossed back over her shoulder as she hurried down the carpeted hall, a small, slim girl with an indefinable air of fragility to her that even the widest of fashionable shoulder-pads couldn't lessen. The reproof stung, though. Catherine was frequently conscious of not pulling her weight—of never having quite pulled her weight—and this bothered her, even upon those frequent occasions when she left at noon on Fridays, or (*Come on, confess it, Cath!*) at ten in the morning (*But not VERY often, really*). At those times she knew she would do no one—certainly not any of her client accounts—any good by sticking around to work when she felt tired, or restless, or simply out of it . . . Nevertheless, she had a horror of being known as "Daddy's Little Girl."

Mostly they said "Charles Chandler's daughter," but in spite of all she tried to do it amounted to the same thing.

"Cathy . . ." Al Prasker emerged from his office, fell into step with her down that wide hallway of wood paneling and glass. "Don't forget the settlement conference at three."

"I'll be there," she promised with her sunniest smile, trying to keep the edge out of her voice, an edge not precisely of annoyance but of harried hurt, for she'd liked Al ever since the days when he'd helped her with her seventh-grade homework in her father's big, rosy-lit study in the pleasant brownstone in Gramercy Park where she'd grown up. *I DON'T need reminding, dammit!* she thought unhappily. *I may come in late and leave early, but I'd never miss a conference, or do anything that would hurt the firm!* As she opened the oak double doors of her father's office suite she felt both unjustly accused and uneasily guilty that Al seemed to regard her as a flake.

Her father was on the phone when she entered his office. He glanced up at her with a smile, a square, pink-faced man with hair that had been the same light sandy brown as hers before it had gone white, and her green eyes. "Hal, let me call you back," he said, as Catherine draped her persimmon-colored duffle-coat over the arm of one of the office's brown leather chairs—despite the beauty of the day it was cold outside. Through the wide windows that comprised the entire rear wall the avenue was a swift-moving current of monochrome grays, splashed along the edges by whirlpools of spring color—ladies' dresses, parked cars, the chipped reds and yellows of hot-dog stands. Around the corner the trees of the park seemed to float weightless in clouds of pink blossom, and Catherine, despite her guilt, had to admit that only the recollection of the settlement conference at three, and of how recently her last unscheduled day off had been, had gotten her here at all.

"That was Hal Sherwood." Charles Chandler put down the phone, looked across at his daughter as she settled into the chair opposite. The office, though not the same one Catherine remembered from her childhood and teenage years—which had been down the street in the old Bradshaw Building—had enough of the things she always associated with her father to make her feel that he'd always been here and always would. His degrees from Harvard and Cornell made pale rectangles of buff on the dark walnut paneling; the antique bottle of carved red lacquer he'd brought back from China for her mother, a bright spot of cinnabar. On his desk her mother's picture and her own stood in heavy silver frames.

"He's coming up from Atlanta tonight," her father went on. "Would you be free to have dinner with us?"

Catherine shook her head. "I can't—I'm sorry. Tom's having a party for the architects of the new building." She smiled wryly. "Another excuse to wine and dine the Planning Commission."

Her father chuckled. "You know, I used to get invited to all those functions." He made a grimace of mock regret—Tom Gunther's parties, generally funded by the firm of Wiegart Development, were famous. "That was before I handed you over to our best client."

"You make it sound like a horse trade."

He answered her kidding smile as she said it, but by the concerned glance he gave her he'd caught the hair-fine line of strain in her voice that told him she wasn't entirely joking. A little hesitantly, he said, "You know, you could do a lot worse than Tom Gunther . . ."

". . . and have," she finished for him, smiling about that too. She knew the episodes that were in his mind.

There was an awkward little silence. But angry and disgusted as he had been at the time—she'd made one or two spectacular mistakes in college— he had never been one to resuscitate a dead issue, particularly ones he knew might still cause her pain or regret. He seemed to have accepted her mistakes as he'd accepted the fact that she hadn't married within a year of being "brought out," nor presented him with grandchildren.

He merely asked, "How about dinner tomorrow night, then?"

"Let me get to my desk, check my calendar," she said, a little too airily, and started to rise. His silver eyebrows pulled down sharply, though he tried to keep his voice casual.

"You're just getting in?"

"I had a late night," she excused herself evasively, not adding, *And about three glasses of wine too many.* It was becoming too easy, she had lately found, to say yes to things that relaxed her when she was slightly uncomfortable about whatever man she happened to be with, as had been the case last night. It had seemed to make sense at the time, but it was something she was beginning to sense she'd have to watch. "And I had some errands to run this morning." She saw the worry still in his sidelong glance, and gave him her brightest smile. "So sue me."

"It's a little late for that," he sighed, rising as she gathered up her coat. "I should have sued you when you were five." And he leaned across to kiss her cheek. "Cathy . . ."

He paused, then moved to sit on a corner of his enormous desk, regarding his only child with concern. Catherine, her coat over her arm, neat and beautiful in her chic black-and-white, felt again the old, recurring sense of helplessness with him, the knowledge that the warmth and love between them had been divided by a wall that seemed to have somehow got built without her knowing it. She only knew it had been there when she'd come back home from college—and later from Europe and the Orient—a little higher, a little thicker every year. There had never been a major fight. It was simply a wall of things unsaid, of subjects not to be brought up, of pain each did not want the other to feel.

After a long hesitation, lawyerlike, to choose his words, he asked gently, "What's up with you?"

The sixty-four thousand dollar question, thought Catherine, remembering that awkward date with Ed last night, and the party she'd gone to with Greg the night before . . . remembering too many men she'd ended up dating because of the vague dread of being alone on a weekend night without anyone asking her anywhere. Dammit, she'd even started going out to discos with Ed, and she didn't even particularly *like* discos. Or Ed, for that matter. Well, Ed wasn't so bad in himself, she temporized. Yet even Tom, certainly her most serious affair in years, so generous, so deferential to her whims, so much everything any reasonable woman should want, gave her a sense of "What's wrong with this picture?"

She almost said, *If I knew what was up with me I'd be halfway home*. But her father, instinctively shying from even that little bit of pain, took the easier way out.

"You don't enjoy the work here?" he asked. "You don't find it stimulating?"

Catherine almost laughed, exasperation mingling with affection at a response that was so typical of

6

him. At the same time, however, she was glad that the real issue hadn't been pulled into the light. If she couldn't define what was wrong, how would he? It would only hurt him again, plague him with the worry that since his wife's death he had somehow failed his child.

She smiled at him. "When I think of corporate law, *stimulating* is not a word that immediately pops into my mind."

Not, she thought, that that was any real excuse for all the late mornings, all the long lunch hours when she'd sit talking to friends in the park, all the early departures because she felt so itchy in her skin she couldn't concentrate . . . But he chuckled at the wryness in her voice and relaxed, accepting the evasion and, as she had been, glad that it hadn't cut any deeper than that. But the little frown stayed in the back of his eyes, as if, from his side of the wall, he knew perfectly well that her actions were not those of a happy woman.

"You know, when you put your mind to it you're a fine corporate lawyer."

"No." Catherine smiled, leaning over to kiss him. "I'm the daughter of a fine corporate lawyer."

Had it been then?

A soft ruffle of sound came to her in her darkness, hollow and weirdly sweet, a series of echoing metallic taps followed after a few moments by other, fainter knocking. Then the distant throb of train wheels rushing over points, like a gust of wind rising . . . fading. On the edge of hearing water gurgled; a smell of worn leather, of beeswax candles, of damp stone and earth. And silence like sleep.

Had she not been so frightened of her weakness,

her pain, her groggy helplessness and the blinding black burden of a terror that never left, she would have slept.

She could, she supposed, have broken her date with Tom Gunther and accepted her father's invitation. They hadn't had dinner together in several weeks—she had been, she guessed, living a little frenetically lately—and once actually *at* a restaurant, the Four Seasons for preference, or some other quiet four-star, or at her father's club, she generally enjoyed these dinners with his business associates. As he'd said, she *was* a fine corporate lawyer, as discontented as she felt with the job. She had a sharp sense of ways and means, a talent for construction, nuance, and implication, and her legal training gave her a keen appreciation of the intricate chess-games of leveraged buy-outs and stock manipulation, of interlocking directorates and who was on the board of what and for what purposes. It was all rather like sitting quietly in a corner of a party, watching who talked to whom and in what order, or catching up on the fine-meshed details of friends' lives.

Or did her failure, her error—whatever it was—go back earlier, to the day her father had taken her to lunch to meet Tom Gunther, the youngest partner of one of the biggest development corporations in the country? Or to the first time, sitting in her office, Tom had interrupted her in the midst of reviewing a right-of-way easement, to ask her out to dinner?

She could, as her father had pointed out, do a lot worse than Tom Gunther.

She'd watched him, briefly, across the atrium ballroom of the Barron Hotel. The place was filled with pink light and opulent if rather conventional arrangements of flowers and catered food, and milling with clients, architects, business associates, the odd member of the City Planning Commission and their assorted dates. Tom, a slim, dark, intent young man with a conscientious tan even this early in the year and an immaculate London-made suit, was giving a guided tour of the ice sculpture in the middle of the lavish buffet table, carved in the shape of the new building that would earn him a seven-digit fee, to the building commissioner and the head of the Irvine Trust. Over the muted hubbub of conversation and well-bred Muzak, Catherine couldn't have heard him if she'd been listening. At the moment she wasn't listening, or even seeking out the sight of him, because Andrew Wiegart Junior's date, enormously to her surprise, had turned out to be Eve Penrith, with whom Catherine had gone to Radcliffe.

Catherine had been shocked at how old Eve looked, and how tired.

"Bad choices," said Eve, shrugging it off as if the slow hell of a disintegrating career and an abusive marriage were matters of no more moment than a mild but inconvenient bout of food poisoning. But beneath the woman's brittle smile, behind her too-ready laugh, Catherine sensed a world of hopeless grief. She'd lost track of Eve in recent years, but her memories of all those nights sitting up till three in their dorm rooms, of conversation and of that slim, sun-browned girl's easy laughter, were like yesterday in her mind. Slipping away from Tom and his business associates, she drew her over into a corner to talk. Eve had badly needed to talk.

"Dammit, the worst of it is I still . . . I don't know whether love is the right word," Eve said, staring down into the cold icy depths of her drink.

In contrast with Catherine's deceptively simple black dress she wore a silvery satin outfit slightly too girlish for her, and didn't wear it well. She had the nervous, haggard look of a woman trying too hard. "But there's something—some feeling of unfinished business. I can't leave it alone. I know I should." Her voice tightened with the effort to remain detached. "They told me just to pretend like he was dead . . ."

Catherine leaned across, to take the bone-thin hand still decorated with a diamond ring. "It'll be all right," she said softly. "Things will turn around."

"You all right?" A hand pressed her shoulder. Looking up, she saw Tom behind her.

"Fine—Eve and I haven't seen each other since college. We have a lot of catching up to do."

It occurred to her that if Eve was dating Andrew Wiegart's son, Tom had probably met her before. But Tom only glanced at her friend, just touching her with his gaze, then turned noncommittally away.

"Good," he said, in his most neutral voice. "I need to talk to you, Cathy."

"Would you excuse us for a minute?"

Eve nodded, her gaze still on her drink, and on whatever it was she saw through it, past it. Tom put a possessive hand on the small of Catherine's back as he steered her over to a quiet place near the paneled stair that ascended to the ballroom's upper level.

"What's with you?"

Catherine looked up at him in surprise. "What do you mean?" Behind them on the stair people continued to enter and leave, businessmen tailored to within an inch of their lives, a sprinkling of conservatively dressed wives keeping a weather-eye out for other wives they knew in the hopes of conversation that didn't involve the words *percentage* or *cost overages*. There was an even larger contingent of ostentatiously beautiful, doll-faced women whom Catherine's friend Jenny claimed the management ordered up by the gross like caviar from Bimbos-R-Us.

Tom gestured impatiently to where Eve remained, quiet at the glass-topped table behind a decorative spray of lilies. "I mean you've been sitting over there listening to her blubber half the night."

Catherine sighed, and shook her head, her eyes going once more to the bowed, defeated figure in the satin dress. "She's going through a rough time, Tom." The memory of Eve's gay courage, of the laughing girl she'd known, hurt her, as if she'd gone to a garden she'd played in as a child and seen it paved over for a parking lot. "We used to be good friends."

"I know her," Tom interrupted bluntly. "She's a lush and she was married to a lush. She's a complete loser."

Anger flickered in her at his tone. She knew Tom abhorred failure, and had run from it all his life. From a blue-collar childhood he'd single-mindedly worked his way up to junior partner in a multi-million-dollar corporation. She shouldn't, she knew, blame him for being what his world had made of him—blame him for having been molded by circumstances which her own father's wealth had spared her—and moreover, at this point a public scene of any kind was the last thing she wanted.

But in spite of herself the edge showed in her voice. "You're very compassionate."

Tom waved the issue away, and gave her his boyish grin. "Don't worry about her," he said dismissively, putting a light, firm hand on her waist. "Come on—you stick with me. There's someone I want you to meet." He started to lead her back toward the buffet table—undoubtedly to meet the building commissioner or someone else influential—and Catherine balked.

This was the side of Tom she liked least, the side she knew her father had no awareness of, or saw differently: the brisk, let's-get-organized business persona he put aside when he'd take her to the theater or to concerts in the park. At times Catherine had the lowering suspicion Tom used her to show off in encounters with business associates. She'd met businessmen like that, who prided themselves on having the most beautiful woman in the room on their arm, even if—like several men here tonight—they had to hire one for the occasion. For some months after she'd met Tom she hadn't thought that was the case with him, because he was proud of her intelligence as well. It had only lately begun to occur to her that his being "proud" of her at all implied the same possessiveness, and it had begun to annoy her.

Or maybe it was just that she was still hurting for Eve.

And so she pulled back.

(*Was it there?*)

Tom looked genuinely surprised. "Look, Tom, I'm sorry," said Catherine contritely. "I'm just not into it tonight."

His slender fingers tightened over hers. "I thought I could count on you." There was hurt in his voice, the charming, little-boy quality that peeked out so often behind that businesslike front.

"You can . . ." she said desperately, feeling guilty now.

"Or maybe I just expect too much."

Dammit, she thought, *now I'm letting HIM down as well as Dad.* She gestured helplessly, trying to get him to lighten up. "This is a party, it isn't brain surgery."

Tom's mouth tightened. For one second, Catherine had the impression that her tiredness, her unwillingness to be sparkling and witty and beautiful—to be Charles Chandler's daughter—for the building commissioner, were to him only another obstacle to be removed or manipulated around. His voice tinged with impatience. "Look, I don't have time for this now." He sounded exactly as if she were making him late for a business meeting, and maybe that was, in fact, the case.

"Frankly," said Catherine, backed into a corner, "I don't like being told whom I can talk to."

But by then he'd lost his temper, too. "Then show better judgment."

"Fine," she said, and removed her fingers from his grasp. "I think I'll call it a night."

He moved in front of her as she walked toward Eve's table where she'd left her dark velvet coat. "That's not an option."

"No?" She was angry now—at his passing judgment on Eve in the first place, at his assumption that he could tell her not to be seen with someone he considered a social liability, and most of all at the mulish look in his face when it had become clear to him that she was going to thwart his desire to show her off as his possession.

She kept her soft voice steady as she said, "Eve, I'm sorry, I'll have to call you tomorrow," as she gathered up her coat, the slithery plum silk of her scarf. But the anger was hot in her as she crossed the room away from the dumbfounded and indignant Tom, and took her departure.

Maybe she could do a lot worse than Tom Gunther, she thought as she crossed the Barron's deserted lobby to the thick plate glass of the door, slipping on her coat as she walked. Maybe he *was* all her father had ever wanted for her: a wealthy, intelligent, and ambitious man who clearly cherished her, who would take care of her, who shared her interests in music and theater and the arts . . . who was good-looking and personable and clean and not a raging campus radical or a spaced-out Parisian poet or a would-be stand-up comic with a coke habit that ran into four digits a week or any of the other types she'd gotten herself involved with . . .

But DAMN it, Catherine thought despairingly, *Dad doesn't have to DATE the man.*

It was just after ten, and the theater rush wouldn't start for nearly an hour. It had drizzled earlier, filling the air with that peculiarly heart-moving city smell of rain, asphalt, and exhaust, and steam from a subway vent a few yards away made a local special-effects zone at the corner. She yelled "Taxi!" but either her voice was too soft—she literally never raised it, something which had pleased her teachers at Miss Farthingale's Academy for Girls when she was little but which cut no ice in the Big Apple—or the driver wasn't paying attention. The vehicle swished by on the water-slick streets, around the corner and away. She ran a few steps after it and stopped, nearly turning her ankle as she stumbled.

Am I really going to have to walk two and a half blocks to Lex on these heels?

"Not having very much luck, are you?" chuckled a man's voice behind her, and she turned. He was medium-short, stocky and dark-haired, hands shoved in the pockets of a light-gray bomber jacket. She had the impression he worked at the hotel, though in fact she didn't give him much thought at all—her mind was still in a turmoil about Eve's problems, and her anger at Tom. In any case he came walking toward her out of the alley that let into the kitchen loading-dock. Though she could barely see him in the shadowy gloom away from the hotel's marquee he gave her a friendly smile. "I'll get one for you, I'm an expert . . . *Taxi!!!*" he bellowed, darting through the silvery cloud of the steam-vent after one that rushed by, though its light was obviously out.

She was looking in her purse for a tip for him when the van came out of the alley.

It turned in front of her and pulled up at the curb, blocking her from the street. Preoccupied with what the hell she was going to do about Tom when he called her up tomorrow—and he'd probably call her at the office, to make matters worse—she didn't think anything of it until the stocky man was beside her, his face hidden in the shadows, only the tips of his curly hair, the pale bone-color of his jacket sleeve, catching the light. She was still in quest of the elusive dollar bill she always kept for the odd tip—later she couldn't *believe* she had been that stupid—when the man's arm went around her, the side door of the van slid open before her, the grating rumble of it almost masking the soft grit of his voice.

"Hey, Carol, you goin' home alone tonight?"

And he threw her into the van.

At the last second her surprise gave way to panic and she twisted against his hold, but he was terrifyingly strong, stronger than she'd expected, and it came to her in a scared splinter of flying thought that though she'd had any number of men put their arms around her, this was the first time she'd discovered what a man's arm was like when it didn't plan to let go.

Then she hit the metal flooring, driving out her scream in a little gasp, and the van was moving even as somebody else—only a stygian shape in the flitting blue blackness of the dark interior—slid the door shut again.

Oh please, God, no . . .

There were two of them plus the driver, but all she could see now were shapes, and the sliding lozenge of a street lamp's glare on a forearm braced on the passenger seat, a forearm tattooed with a red-and-blue dragon whose claws and mouth embraced the hairy back of a hand. Her eyes were glued to that dragon as her mind stalled, numb with shock and terror like a rabbit frozen in a car's headlights.

. . . how could I be that stupid?

. . . no, please . . .

. . . diamonds, my earrings are diamonds, maybe they'll take my earrings and let me go . . .

She knew already they weren't going to let her go till they were done.

The stocky man shoved her back against the side wall of the van, one hand effortlessly holding both her wrists behind her, his body pressing hers. She smelled the sweat in his shirt, some kind of cheap after-shave, the burned tobacco on his breath as he whispered over and over, "That's a girl—that's a girl— You know what happens to little girls with big mouths?"

There was a soft metallic click. The van rocked, and a flick of streetlight caught on a six-inch leaf of shining steel in the dragon hand. "You're about to find out."

"Carol," whispered the caressing voice in her ear, "you got to remember to keep your mouth shut from now on."

Panicked, frozen, she managed to whisper, "My name isn't Carol."

"*Shut up!*" His hand grabbed the front of her coat, slammed her back against the metal wall, banging her head.

The other man's body blocked the whisk of passing lights; she sensed rather than saw the knife.

"You'll remember now," gritted that soft voice. "And every time you look in a mirror . . ."

Two

THE faint clanging spoke again, like strange and random bells.

Lying in darkness, lying in pain—pain that localized in her shoulders and back and belly, pain that stabbed her with the clouded reminiscence of ten times greater agony every time she drew breath—Catherine tried to remember just at what point she could have called a halt to the whole proceedings and walked away safe. There had to have been something . . .

It was like trying to pick up water in her hand. Thoughts and memories—the gritty monochrome vista of the Avenue of the Americas seen through her father's window, her own image in the mirror back at her apartment as she spent the usual careful hour with her makeup; the saccharine Muzak and impersonal chatter of the party and the weary grief in Eve's tired eyes—spun away like brown leaves from the seat of a whirled merry-go-round, tumbling into darkness.

She'd been conscious when they'd thrown her out of the van. It had to have been in Central Park, with its woodland cold and sinister whispers. Lying

in the wet grass she'd had the vague impression of
headlights sweeping across her body, of traffic
noises somewhere near. She remembered blind
blackness, pain such as she'd never experienced;
the damp cold of the sodden ground soaking the
warmth from her body and the slow trickle away
from her of what little strength she'd had left. She
remembered, as if remembering some chasm-deep
dream, the realization that she was dying . . .

She could not decide whether the rest of it was
a dream or not.

This place . . .

She was warm—she lay on something soft. Her
hand, when she moved it, felt the change of
textures, soft cotton, old wool stitched with leather,
crochet-work . . . a patched quilt? Those impres-
sions too whirled away, sleep enfolded her.

"No!" She woke up with a cry, her hands flying
up, and the stab of pain in her ribs brought back
the black horror of her dream again. Her mouth
hurt, swollen and half numb; something was
covering her eyes—she couldn't see . . . She
thought, *What if they still have me* . . . "No . . ."

"You're safe," said a voice softly. "You're safe
now."

Everything within her flinched with terror at the
sound of an unknown voice—a man's voice. But it
was the gentlest, the kindest voice she had ever
heard.

"Where am I?"

"No one will hurt you," said the voice, deep and
slightly gritty in texture: granite and silk. "You're
safe here."

"Am I in a hospital?" The smell of the place was
not a hospital smell. She turned her head a little,

as if she could see him where she knew he had to be, sitting or standing to her left and a little behind her.

"No," replied the voice gently. "But you're going to be all right."

"Why aren't I in a hospital?" She felt her panic rising at the thought of being this weak, this alone . . . at the thought of being in anyone's power.

"You were bleeding. There was no time."

She thrust from her that cold little seed of half-memory, the knowledge, as she'd felt her consciousness fraying away into the wet darkness, that she was dying. What had happened after that?

Her voice trembled and she fought to steady it. "What did they do?" She raised one hand, fumbled at her face. As she'd suspected, her head was swathed in bandages. Panic struck her again, panic now not at the past—at the dreams—but at the future. "My eyes . . ."

"Your eyes are not hurt."

Then why cover them? she wondered desperately. *Why are you lying to me?*

But it was the voice of one who does not know how to lie.

In the clouded hours—days?—of darkness and delirium, of the memories of the men dragging her into the van, the endless, hideous recurrent dreams of being kicked and hammered, of the silver glint of the knife, she had felt nothing but fear. It had seemed to her that she would never trust anyone—not her father, not Tom, not fate, not God—again.

But she trusted that voice.

She slept.

It had to have been him, she thought, in the silken cocoon of her dreams. The memory never surfaced in wakefulness, for it was not a conscious memory, but unconscious, she remembered the susurrance of a cloak hem over grass, and the muffled whisper of leather, metal, cloth. The pain had been almost gone then, swallowed up in a merciful numbness, but she'd been very cold. She thought he'd picked her up like a child and carried her—down a hill, through leaves that brushed wetly against her legs—into someplace where she'd felt steamy warmth against the raw flesh of her face . . .

Carried her for a long way. She'd been sliding in and out of even that thread of awareness. Sometimes she thought there had been stairs, an endless descending spiral that chimed faintly metallic under the padded weight of his boots. Sometimes echoes spoke to one another, the far-off voices of water, the thud of machinery and the clattering pulse-beat of a train. Sometimes silence, broken only by that dim, didactic clanking that even now pursued her into the chasm of her dreams, and like an intermittently gleaming chain, drew her out again.

She heard the rustle of clothing as she came back to consciousness, the stiff creak of belt leather and the almost soundless tread of feet. Whoever was in the room moved with an almost abnormal quiet, but blindness—however produced—and fear made her senses acute, and she turned her head swiftly on the yielding chaos of pillows, the motion bringing dizziness and a sickening throb to her swollen face.

"Who's here?" she asked, trying to believe it wasn't the men in the van come back, trying to believe what had happened to her wouldn't happen again. "*Who are you?*"

There was perceptible hesitation. Then he said,

"Vincent," the voice she had known, had trusted, before. He came closer, kneeling, she thought, next to her. He went on, "My father and I treated your injuries. You have broken ribs. You need to rest, to be still."

"Where am I?" She reached out toward him, wanting to touch something human, to know something more than a voice, but he was just beyond her reach, and did not take her hand. Weak, it fell back on the quilt, encountering a patch of fur in its pattern, a triangle of what felt like velvet, a square of lace.

"You are where no one can hurt you," said Vincent, and in the soft, scratchy bronze of his tones she heard that this fact, and not any specific whereabouts, was the important thing, both to him and to her.

But how can I be sure? And why won't you tell me . . . ?

"Tell me your name."

As if it were something that mattered whom she gave it to, whom she trusted it with, she hesitated, then said, "Catherine."

"Catherine," he repeated softly. "Try to rest. If you need anything I'll be close by. Don't be afraid. Please, don't be afraid."

It was more than the beauty of his voice, she thought; it was some quality of caring, as if the thing that truly most concerned him was that, trapped as she was in darkness and despair, she at least could feel that she need have no fear. But that was a thing impossible to her now—impossible, she thought, ever again. She felt once more for his hand, and heard him move, as if he meant to take it, then draw back.

In a tiny voice she stammered, "I'll try."

* * *

Vincent waited, sitting beside her in silence, until she slept. This room—his own—was dimly illuminated by a myriad of candles in holders of silver or glass, by old mended lamps of Tiffany work, by the dim embers in a low, round hearth and by an eerie, colored glow which never changed. In the golden light he studied the sleeping girl's hands: small and square like a child's, well cared for, the hands of one who has never worked. But strong hands, quick-looking, not useless as they lay on the faded colors of the quilts.

Catherine.

An alien creature from an alien world.

His heart ached with pity. Gently he drew the covers up over her, gathered the smoke-stained wool of his cloaklike sleeved mantle about him, and left the room.

In the tunnels the soft, never-ceasing tap and clatter was louder, echoing weirdly in the low vaults of brickwork, the raw wet faces of stone. It was a sound he had grown up with, a kind of heartbeat, reassuring to him even in sleep. Thinking about the girl—about the dark shape lying huddled in the gloom of the park with the blonde spill of her hair hiding her face, the smell of her blood mingling with the heavy scent of the drenched grass—he barely glanced about him as he descended a short flight of discolored brick steps into the darkness of a tunnel, passed through one corner of a great rock-hewn chamber where steam from pipes far overhead drifted in impenetrable gloom, and through another door.

His father was where he thought he'd be, in his own room, reading a book.

Father's room was two stories high, roughly

circular and vaulted, and filled—floor to ceiling on
one rough stone wall and heaped in stacks, pillars,
pyramids between every other piece of its battered
old furnishings—with books. Old encyclopedias and
yellowing 'thirties pulps, Everyman's Classic
Libraries sold to the rich by the yard in cured
leather and gold, crumbling old novels, saints' lives
and Hegel, bright-covered Book Club editions
bought to be thrown away, Shakespeare, Donne,
Cervantes and paperback self-help, the gleanings
of a thousand libraries, they rose in shadowy pillars
around Vincent as he passed through the little
vestibule with its scarred stone caryatids and
crumbling pillars and down the short iron-railed
steps to the main chamber. Across the rear of the
room at the height of about twelve feet ran a
wooden balcony, which Vincent and some of the
others had built years ago out of scrap lumber and
the carved oak balustrades salvaged from a torn-
down church. From the underside of this depended
half a dozen oil lamps and crude chandeliers,
which flooded the room with a burnished topaz
glow. In spite of the shadows which reigned there
Vincent noted in passing that not only were all the
bookshelves above the balcony tightly packed now
to the inward curve of the vaulted ceiling, but the
balcony itself was getting stacked with Father's
newest acquisitions. Something else was going to
have to be done fairly soon.

It was physically difficult for Vincent to smile,
but there was rueful amusement in his inner sigh
and the shake of his head.

Standing on that balcony beneath the candles of
an old bronze lamp, book in hand and head bowed
over it in thought, was his father.

Father was a short, square man, his hair and his

close-clipped beard grizzled to the color of rusted steel. His eyes, behind an ancient pair of steel-rimmed reading glasses, were gray-blue, shrewd and sharp as he turned to look down when Vincent entered the room.

"Is she awake?"

It was cold in Father's rooms, as it was in most of the tunnels. The elderly man wore a pair of old brown gloves with the fingers cut out of them, and thick gray socks cross-gaitered with leather straps over his wrists and forearms. His robes, like Vincent's clothes, were soft old leather and pieces patched and quilted together from old coats and suits, worn and faded with age and washing; at the neck the gray pullover showed, which he had on underneath.

Vincent nodded. "She's very frightened."

"Vincent, how could you?" Leaning heavily on the balustrade, his long robe rustling, Father limped down the steps—worn granite pulpit-steps from that same old church—and pulled off his glasses to look up at his tall adopted son. "How could you bring a stranger here, to where we live? You ignored our most important rule."

"But there was no other way," said Vincent in his low, patient voice. Father was afraid, and had good right to be. But Father had not seen the girl—Catherine—as he had, dumped in one of the loneliest corners of the park. Vincent knew the park, knew the rhythms of its nights; the routes and pace of the few police patrols, the ebb and flow of those who walked its hours of darkness. He knew no one would have come.

He suspected his father did, too.

The old man turned, looking up at him, in his eyes an anger born of distrust and worry. "Do you know what they'd do to you if they caught you up there?" he asked. "Or found you down here? They'd kill you . . . or lock you up and make you wish you were dead."

Vincent knew that was true, too.

Distantly the soft metallic knocking sounded, clearer here than in Vincent's rooms; a pause, then higher, farther, a reply. Father shook his head. "How could you?" he repeated.

"I know that," Vincent replied softly. "But there was no other way. How could I have turned my back on her and left her there?"

Under the grizzled mustache Father's mouth tightened. Without a word he collected his stick from its usual resting place beside his tattered tapestry armchair, and with its help limped to where his old medical bag lay on the corner of a grotesque Victorian Gothic sideboard, one of the few horizontal surfaces in the room not heaped with moldering tomes. Even his limp was strong and concise.

"Make sure she takes these to prevent infection." He produced from the depths of the bag a little plastic bottle containing half a dozen tetracycline capsules.

"I'll make sure."

"I was saving them for an emergency," he added reproachfully. "You know how difficult they were to obtain."

"Father, try to understand," said Vincent. "This was an emergency. She would have died."

The old man looked away, the fear he lived with warring in his blunt features with his natural compassion, his anger at a world that would do, to that girl he'd stitched together yesterday, what had obviously been done. "All right," he said quietly.

"We'll help her regain her strength." He glanced back up at Vincent. "But the moment she's ready to leave, you must get her out of here. And Vincent . . ." he added. "Don't tell her *anything*."

"I won't," said his son. "Don't worry, Father. It won't be very long. She's already starting to heal."

Father sighed. "I hope so." He stood for a moment, looking up into Vincent's face. "You have the soul of a doctor," he said, almost wonderingly, then chuckled to himself with ironic humor. "When I studied medicine they wouldn't admit minorities—or women. I wonder what they would have done with you?" He shuddered, as if he had a suspicion. "Let's not even think about it."

And reaching up, he took Vincent's head between his hands and kissed him gently on the forehead.

"Vincent, tell me," said Catherine, "where are we?" Though still sickeningly weak, she had wakened feeling better. The dreamy grogginess had given way to lassitude, as if her arms and legs were swathed in sheet-lead, exhausting to lift or move. Others had been there besides Vincent, other voices identifiable through the darkness of her bandaged eyes; a crisp, vaguely British voice and deft hands that had checked the bruises on her side; a woman who had changed the soft, patched homespun nightgown she wore, and had helped her to the washroom adjacent to the chamber where she lay.

But it was Vincent who had been with her when she'd waked this time, Vincent who'd spoken to her in that deep, gentle voice, who'd brought her soup and fed her when her own hands were too shaky with weakness, exhaustion, and loss of blood to hold the spoon.

He didn't reply. In his silence she heard the swift rush of a train going by overhead somewhere, and then, like the murmurous echo of its sound, the eternal metallic tapping returned.

"Somewhere there's an elevated train," she persisted. "Are we in Brooklyn? Queens?" She doubted they (*they who?*) could be keeping her in Manhattan undetected. Or could they? How long had she been missing? Why hadn't anyone begun to search?

Vincent sounded troubled. "No—not Brooklyn or Queens."

"Am I still in New York at all?" She knew she should have been more frightened now than she was. For all she knew she was blind, in the power of people she didn't know, in a place she couldn't identify and was far too weak to even try to escape . . . And yet, weirdly, she felt more curious than afraid. Vincent would not let anything happen to her. That much she knew.

"Vincent, please," she murmured through numbed and swollen lips. "Tell me where we are."

There was the muted clink of a spoon on the soup bowl he held as he moved uncomfortably. Then, "I have to keep it a secret."

"Why?"

Another long hesitation, while he picked out what he could say that would be neither a lie nor a betrayal. His voice had a slight thickness to some of its sounds, not quite a lisp or a slur, but an impediment of some kind. It did nothing to alter the beauty of it, the quality of endless strength. At length he replied, "Because—a lot of good people depend on this place for safety."

When she had first wakened, terrified in darkness and too weak to lift her hand, she had thought of escape; had listened around her, trying to piece together something that might help her. But beyond the pervasive smell of dampness and smoke, candlewax and what must be kerosene—beyond the omnipresent, chiming tap and rattle of metal in the distance, the occasional rise and fall of a passing train, she had heard nothing: no telephone, no traffic noise, no tinny subvibration of radio or TV. She couldn't remember how long it had been since she'd been in a place that didn't have that ubiquitous background tapestry of half-heard sound.

But that alienness, too, frightened her less than it had. *Good people*, he had said, and she believed him.

"Vincent, I'll keep your secret."

In his silence she could almost feel the division of his mind.

"And that tapping," she added softly, uneasily. "It never stops."

"It's people talking to each other," replied Vincent. "Tapping on the master pipes."

"You mean messages?" She'd heard of men doing it in prisons—as a child she and a visiting cousin had experimented with the concept and had plumbers going over the house for weeks.

In his throat he made a noise of assent.

"Vincent, please . . . tell me."

She heard him sigh.

"We're below the city," he said. "Below the subways. There's a whole world of tunnels and chambers that most people don't even know exists. There are no maps to where we are. It's a forgotten place. But it's warm, and it's safe, and we have all the room we need."

Half-formulated memories of being carried down

through darkness stirred in her mind, the echo of dripping water, the damp breath of steam. The silence.

"So we live here," he went on quietly, "and we try to live as well as we can, and we try to take care of each other. It's our city, down here."

A city without light, she thought. No, she heard them moving about, Father and the woman, as if they could see—smelled smoke and candles and fuel . . . A city without interference. A city without electricity, or proper medical facilities—this was something which had worried her, in spite of the antibiotics Vincent had given her. A city without the kind of men who'd thrown her into the black van.

A city of outcasts?

"And you?" she asked. "What are you doing down here? Why are you here?"

There was an even longer silence. At last he said slowly, painfully, "I was a baby . . . abandoned, left to die. Someone found me, brought me here, to the man who became my father."

She remembered the decisive British voice, through the haze of grogginess and pain, the deft skill with the bandages. Remembered Vincent saying, "Father."

Love replaced the pain in the deep voice as Vincent went on, "He took me, he raised me . . . he taught me everything. He named me Vincent." There was a soft sound, like a deep chuckle. "That's where I was found, near the hospital—St. Vincent's. Here," he added softly. "This will get cold." The tip of the spoon touched her lips.

Did that account, she wondered, for the trust she felt for him, for that quality of innocence, of honesty, that underlay the velvet strength of his voice? The fact that he'd been brought up in this other world—if it *was* another world, as he said. She had, she told herself, sipping at the broth, only his word to go on. There was absolutely nothing to prove that he wasn't lying about everything he said.

Yet why would he lie?

Why would three men shove some woman they'd never met into a van, smash her to pieces like demented children breaking up a piece of furniture and throw her out to die?

Pain came back, almost choking her—not the pain of her chipped ribs, her swollen, throbbing face, but an inner pain: the pain of having all trust, all safety she had ever felt, dissolve beneath her like wave-washed sand. She whispered desperately, "I—I don't know what to believe . . ."

The spoon touched her lips again; Vincent's voice was deep with compassion. "Believe it," he said softly, as if he understood how deeply she needed to be able to believe something. "It's all true."

She reached up to steady the spoon, and for the first time her hand came in contact with his.

Huge, powerful, covered with long coarse hair and armed with hooked inch-long claws, it was not a human hand.

Three

Investigators say they will continue the seven-day-old search for Catherine Chandler, who disappeared April 12. Miss Chandler, fashionable and popular East Side deb and daughter of the senior partner of the law firm of Chandler and Prasker, was last seen leaving a party at the Barron Hotel in midtown Manhattan last Monday night at 10:30 p.m.

Captain John Hermann of the NYPD, who is in charge of the case, reports that the girl's purse was found beside a path near the Central Park Reservoir the following morning, emptied of cash and stained with blood. Neither Miss Chandler's father nor her boyfriend, noted real estate developer Tom Gunther, were available for comment.

There was a picture.

"She said she'd been at a party," remarked Vincent softly, and Father's sharp blue eyes flicked up to him from the folded newspaper he held in his hands, annoyed, as if to ask if that was all he had to say.

"They don't let their daughters go missing without a fuss, those lawyers and bankers and stockbrokers of the East Side," said the old man dourly. "Or do much of anything else, for that matter . . . I know," he added, with the bitterness of some old memory shading the edges of his voice. "It means that every day she's here increases our danger."

"And how should it not?" inquired Vincent, cocking his head a little to look down at the sturdy old man standing before him in the halo of the candles on the study's octagonal mahogany desk. "If she were your daughter, would you not uproot the very foundations of the city to find her?"

Father grunted. "All very well, unless one happens to be living among those foundations." He removed his reading glasses, dropped them onto the desk and limped around it to take his chair. "She must go, Vincent."

"She'll be well enough to leave in a few days," said his son soothingly. Father's only reply was a noncommittal growl, and Vincent left him sitting at his desk, still perusing the offending newspaper with worried eyes.

Had it been only seven days?

Her strength was slow in returning, though she could be up and down for a few minutes at a time now. She had been badly beaten. Vincent had no conception why anyone would do this to a woman—or to anyone, for that matter— though he knew perfectly well that they did. The books he had read, the newspapers—collected by the Tunnel children from every garbage can in the city—which Father regularly received from the world above, were full of such matters, and the people he had talked to in the Tunnels, the people who had once lived Above, spoke of it, if not calmly, at least philosophically.

"Happens all the time, Vincent," Winslow had said, turning from him to the bigger of his two anvils, over which a hunk of steel—part of a '72 Buick's door-panel, in fact—lay. Winslow was a big black man, bearded and mostly bald. Like Vincent he had grown up in the Tunnels, but had spent seven or eight years living Above.

In the heat of his workshop he was stripped to the waist and his muscles gleamed with sweat as he methodically began pounding the panel flat. On the floor in one corner of the rock-cut room lay a pile of such roughly straightened pieces of iron and steel, for repairing pipes and making the doors and traps, the false entrances and sliding grilles, that protected the inner tunnels from chance incursion from without. In another corner old car parts, pots and pans too corroded at the bottom for use, and a couple of dented steel oil-drums half-filled with empty beer cans and food cans were heaped. Old coffee cans and mayonnaise jars filled with nails, screws, rivets and bolts of various sizes, all neatly graded, lined the shelves above the workbench; the ruddy glow of a small forge added its light to the ochre glow of four or five kerosene lamps set on the benches or hanging on the walls.

Vincent had waited—this was two or three days ago—arms folded under his heavy mantle, leaning one broad shoulder in the doorway, until the clanging of hammer on steel had ceased and the blacksmith paused for breath.

"I know it happens all the time," he'd said. "But *why* does it happen all the time?"

Winslow shrugged, his gloved hands shifting their grip on the tools. "Drugs, a lot of it," he replied, and the glint of ancient angers flickered in his brown eyes.

Vincent shook his head. Drugs were another thing he knew existed but had never understood the why of.

"Or money. People get crazy over a couple of dollars."

"It makes no sense."

Winslow's teeth flashed whitely in the red light from the forge. "If it made sense, you think I'd be livin' down here? You ever figure out the why of it," he added, gesturing with his hammer as he turned back to his work again, "you be sure to tell somebody—they'll be glad to know up there."

Mary, the Tunnel midwife, had been slightly more helpful. She was a small, sturdy woman in her forties, her long blonde hair turning gray. It was she who looked after the children of the Tunnels, who had split the nursing of Catherine with Vincent even as she had covered for him in his own duties as the children's teacher. Vincent had been reading to Catherine—Dickens' *Great Expectations*, one of his own favorites—and she had fallen asleep to the sound of his voice. He had sat for a long time after that, looking down at the bandage-swathed face against the crochet-work of the pillow covers, until Mary appeared at the top of the steps leading up to the vestibule and he'd gone up to speak with her, and had asked her the same question he'd put to Winslow.

"It's a—a craziness," she'd said slowly, her lined face troubled, her worn hands, callused from needle and pestle and washboard, rubbing slowly over the thick russet knit of her sleeves. "Even laboratory rats, you know, if you put too many of them together in one cage—even if there's enough food for all—will start killing and eating one another out of . . . a kind of rage, I think." She looked up at him, her eyes sad. She had seen Catherine when Vincent had brought her in. "So many people up there have nowhere to go."

He thought of that now, as he passed through the small brick vestibule where that conversation had taken place, and stood at the top of the steps leading down into his room.

Catherine was sitting on the edge of the bed, her hands folded and her bandaged head bowed. To him she looked very small in the folds of the much-washed and -mended nightgown; small, and very alone. Yet there was no terror in the way she sat, no huddled fear. Without speaking, holding to the shadows as was his eternal instinct, he studied the lines of her slim square shoulders, her slender back. Lines of strength, even bent as they were now with despair, just as her voice, soft and low and familiar to him as those he had heard all of his life, had never, in all the week of their conversations, been whining, or petulant, or weak.

There was something in her that reminded him of the finest gold, in its warmth and elemental purity, if anything could be said to be comparable to a human soul—if anything could be said to be comparable to her.

She raised her head, the bandages over her eyes darkened and wet; when she spoke there was bitterness in her voice. "I know you're there," she said. "You can come in."

She spoke as if at that moment she hated him,

though he sensed that her hatred was reserved for other things: for her pain, for her helplessness, for her shattered trust in life that had cut her open like broken glass.

Gently, as if he had not heard the bitterness in her voice, he said, "I'll read to you," and she turned her face away, as if through the bandages she could see where he stood.

"It won't help."

"It might," said Vincent. "We can finish *Great Expectations*. Do you remember how it ends?"

She shook her head, refusing to have her pain quieted now, as he had quieted it during the long days of her convalescence. "Vincent, I'm frightened. I'm worried."

He wanted to go to her, to hold her for comfort, but after the single time she had touched his hand while he held the spoon for her, had pulled back her fingers in horrified alarm, he had never gotten near enough to her to permit even accidental physical contact. Her gasp of shock had been enough. But someone ought to. Words were not what she needed, and he knew of none that would heal a wound as deep as the ones inflicted upon her.

All he could say was "I know. I can feel it . . . You're getting your strength back." He felt very helpless, helpless as he never had before. "I'll get you some tea," he offered. "The herb tea that you liked."

Her voice was small and tight. "All right."

His retreat from the room was hastier than he had planned.

This time of the day—midafternoon, in the world Above—the children were usually scattered everywhere about the deep mazes that laced the gray

Manhattan bedrock, taking a few hours to explore and play between their lessons and their evening chores. But Vincent knew well the places they played—he had played there himself as a child, for one thing, and for another he routinely patrolled them, knowing all the hazards of the world underground. It didn't take him long to locate two or three of the mid-sized kids, skateboarding down The Reach, a long stretch of abandoned storm-drain that offered nearly two hundred feet of unbroken floor, a rarity underground.

The kids—Dustin, Miranda, and Kipper—greeted him with delight, he being not only their unofficial guardian and teacher in the arts of reading but a storyteller and hide-and-seek player of rare and ferocious abandon. 'Randa, who of the three knew the tunnels best, had promised to help Mary with her herbs before supper, and Dustin, at seven, Vincent knew to be slightly too young to undertake a long expedition—a judgment call the little boy disagreed with mightily—but Kipper allowed as how he'd be willing to undertake the quest.

"Take this tunnel three platforms down," Vincent directed, pointing off down the left-hand fork of The Reach's primary crossing-main. "Go right up the next tunnel to the first ladder and start climbing . . ."

"And that'll be Chinatown?" Kipper, aged nine, had been in the Tunnels three years after one of the Helpers—a stout, white-haired man who ran a barbershop near Times Square—had found the boy hiding in a dumpster with cigarette burns all over his arms, refusing to go home.

"Unless you take the wrong tunnel," said Vincent gravely. "If you do, you *could* end up in China." It usually took kids a couple of years to

learn even the relatively small area in which most
denizens of the subterranean world made their
homes, and there were adults who'd spent five
years, or ten, in the Tunnels without learning more
than their own immediate area, and how to get
from there to certain specific points—the nearest
wells, the ladders which led up to the cellars of
Helpers, the chambers of friends. Most of the
young men knew the perimeter of the more inhabited areas, from patrolling the entrances, but the
entrances themselves were frequently changed.
Vincent was one of the few who knew all of New
York: every steam vent, every manhole, every
access tube and disused drain. He knew the
secondary and tertiary routes, and ways to get from
one section of the deeper levels to another where
there weren't always tunnels to connect them;
knew every secret gate, every underground spring
and ancient, sunken lagoon. From the Painted
Tunnels to the Chamber of Winds he prowled them
endlessly, far beyond the usual habitations of those
who lived Below, a lonely kingdom of solitude and
night.

But he knew Kipper well enough to be sure the
boy would have no problems on an easy run down
to Chinatown and back.

The boy grinned at him cockily. "Okay—but this
one's going to cost you." And he scrambled down
the few steel rungs into the crossing tunnel and
was gone in a swirl of leather, patchwork, and
rags.

Slowly, Catherine looked around her.

After over a week without sight, or with only the
dimness visible through her eyelids under the
bandages, even the candlelight seemed bright;

shocking, as the touch of air on her skin was almost painful.

With shaking fingers, she pulled the last of the bandages away.

Up until the last moment, in spite of Vincent's repeated reassurances that her eyes had not been harmed—not been touched—she had feared that something was wrong with her sight. Why else would they have kept her eyes bandaged?

But in that, it seemed, she could trust him as well.

There was a rawness to that thought, too, like the air on the hurtingly tender skin of her face. She'd thought she was never going to trust anyone, or anything, again.

Vincent had said that this was his room. Now she looked around it, saw it for the first time, though bits of it had gradually become familiar to her touch as she'd been able to get up and move around in the last day or so. But it was not as she had expected.

And it was everything that deep, soft voice, with its compassion and its strength, had implied.

There were candles everywhere, the air molten with their light and pervaded with smoke and beeswax. By the resinous glow she saw the bed where she had lain, with its muted quilts of patchwork, leather and fur, its colored afghans, its worn and mended linen. A carved chair with a leather seat; a marble caryatid with a beautiful, archaic face, salvaged off some long-demolished facade; a table piled with books; a poster of Einstein eating a lollypop, of John Lennon, of Amelia Earhart and Igor Stravinsky. A great fan-shaped window of stained glass, apricot and blue, looked out onto some place lit with the muted glow of a hundred kerosene lamps. A few embers still burned in a round hearth whose mantle—clearly salvaged from some torn-down brownstone of her grandparents' vintage and supported by two marble fauns—held an assorted clutter of music boxes, papers, a bronze souvenir model of the Empire State Building and a stack of Theodore Sturgeon paperbacks.

With its rock walls, its half-obscured colors and varied textures, it was a room of great comfort, physical, intellectual, and emotional; the room of a man at peace with himself.

He had grown up here, she remembered. He had been abandoned—as a baby, he'd said. For a moment, looking around her, she forgot her own fears, her own growing dreads, and thought about what it would have been like, to be a small child and to think about the fact that the first thing your parents had done with you was to get rid of you.

And in spite of all that, he had grown up to be the man Vincent clearly was.

Thinking about that eased the bitterness inside her, and for a few moments almost abated the dread.

And then the fear returned.

It had been with her from the start, when she'd been worried about her eyes. It had grown, when Vincent had spoken—guardedly, but less guardedly than he knew—of how life was lived Below. Of Father's skill as a doctor, in spite of difficult and frequently primitive conditions; of how those who lived Below had to scavenge for what they used, living on the cast-offs of the opulent city on which they had turned their backs, and which had turned its back on them. The fact that there had been so few antibiotics in that bottle Father had given Vincent had told its own tale, like a whispered reminder every time she put her hands to her bandaged face, and had felt the engorged tenderness of the flesh beneath the wrappings.

And behind that, down in the bottomless black crack of nightmare, a man's voice whispering, *You'll remember now and every time you look in a mirror,* and the streetlight flashing on a blade in a tattooed hand.

Hardly daring to, she put her hands to her face.

It was difficult to tell anything. The flesh was still swollen and agonizingly tender to her touch, but she knew it shouldn't feel like that.

She got to her feet, stumbling, her knees still weak and shaky. The floor was thick with carpets—Aubussons and Persians worn nearly colorless, soft beneath her bare feet. She stumbled to the desk, to the dressing table, hunting for a mirror with growing panic. It was almost as if, perversely, the desk, the mantle, the tables contained everything but that, and her mind touched briefly on that seemingly deliberate omission and then skimmed past like a frightened bird.

Her movements grew more frantic as she searched, as she grew desperate to know the worst . . . to know where she stood. To know the truth. *Dammit, anything . . .*

Among the clutter on the mantle she finally found the shallow silver bowl of a car headlight's reflector, dented on the outside but polished within like glass. Her hands fumbled with it, angling it to the soft aureate radiance of the Tiffany lamps.

Her breath caught in half a whisper, half a cry. "Oh, God!"

It was worse than she'd feared.

Much worse.

Even allowing for the distortion of the silver

mirror, even allowing for the swelling that lingered after a week, the fading bruises, the wrinkled pallor of skin long kept from air and the flattened, pulled-back frame of her unwashed hair . . .

Bristling with sutures, the knife cuts crisscrossed her face in scabbed black lines like nightmare graffiti. Both cheeks were disfigured with long, forking slashes like crooked Y's, a cut pulled one side of her upper lip out of shape, another ran over her forehead, splitting one eyebrow. Yet another ran past her left ear and down onto the jaw. She wanted to scream and couldn't, could only stare with despairing horror, frozen and sickened, gazing back at that face—it *had* to be somebody else's face!—white and puffy and hideous, with its scribbled black lines and its wide, staring green eyes.

"Catherine!"

It was Vincent's voice, wrung with compassion and concern. But behind her in the distorted reflector she saw another face, and this time she did scream.

It was the face of a beast.

A freak, a monstrosity, he was behind her as she turned: well over six feet tall, massively built, with an animal's flattened nose and fanged muzzle framed in a long, honey-colored tangle of mane. Scared, shocked, with a cry she flung the reflector at him. Its edge caught him on the forehead, leaving a crescent of blood. He drew back with a snarl of pain and she saw the flash of his fangs. Then he put up his hand, the clawed and hairy paw she had felt—she had convinced herself that she had not felt—some days ago, to cover his face in mortification and shame. Turning quickly, he fled from the room.

Four

I have never regretted what I am," said Vincent softly. "Until now."

I'm sorry had already been said. He had come back, drawn by her weeping—it wasn't until later that she thought about how much courage that in itself must have taken, after her initial reaction of horror at something that was clearly not his fault. It was as if he had known that her tears, as she lay stretched facedown on his bed, had not been for herself, not tears of horror and self-pity at her own situation, but tears of shame for what she had done to him.

And maybe he had known. When he spoke, he spoke as if the incident were forgotten, as if all that had passed between them had been unmarred—the conversations of the past week; the nights she had waked crying from nightmares, when he had stolen in softly as some giant cat to talk to her, to read to her, to tell her the stories he told the children; the days when he'd coax out of her her own stories, of the friends she'd known in college, or met in her travels through Italy and France.

But he stood now in the doorway, where the

shadows hid him, and had drawn up the hood that hung on the back of the mantle he wore over his clothes, a great sleeveless coat of leather and patchwork rags against the Tunnels' chill, so that his face was half-concealed.

"How?" she asked, gazing across at the tall, massive shape, veiled in dimness save where the light lay across his folded hands, with their long reddish hair and heavy claws. "How did this happen to you?" She no longer thought of him, as she had for that terrible instant of shock, as a freak or a monster—only a friend to whom something dreadful had happened, something that had left him far more marked than she.

His head moved a little in the concealing hood. "I don't know." The voice was the same, deep and beautiful, a voice she would hear in her dreams, she already knew, if she lived to be ninety years old. "I have ideas, but I'll never know." The enormous hands started a gesture, but left it unmade. The light caught the pointed, yellowish claws. "I was born . . . and I survived."

He said it simply, as the only facts that mattered, like sketch lines enclosing the bitter loneliness of being forever exiled to the Tunnels for fear of what the world Above would do to such as he. The knowledge that he was, and always would be, an outsider.

And, in a way, they *were* the only things that mattered. He was what he was—the compassion, the tireless patience and care he had given her, the gentleness and the strength—and she could not imagine his being other than what he was.

Or, now that she saw him, looking other than he did.

For he was not ugly. He reminded her, more

than anything else, of a great tawny lion, with a lion's size and power and soundless grace. Like Aslan, she thought, in the C. S. Lewis novels she'd loved as a child. Only his eyes, clear sapphire blue under a slanting topaz bristle of brow, were the eyes of a man—save that she knew few men whose eyes held that innocent calm.

Softly the pipes clanked their endless rhythm, a whispered query, a staccato reply. With a slight hesitation, as if he still feared to frighten her, Vincent stepped forward, and she saw that he had been standing with a rolled-up bundle of clothes beneath his arm, half-hidden by his mantle. He let them fall to the bed by her side, and she recognized the bulky velvet coat she'd worn to Tom's party at the Barron, the elegantly simple black dress she'd spent days shopping for, the high heeled black shoes and long plum-colored scarf. The dress had been cleaned of blood, and mended with careful, even stitches. She could barely bring herself to look at it, remembering.

"It's time for you to go back."

She hadn't thought the idea of going back would hit her like that, a sickening throb of fear, like a blow with a baseball bat to the pit of the stomach. She looked up at him in silence, feeling tears heat her eyes; feeling, it seemed, every rip and scar and suture of her ruined face. Feeling that wherever she went, that black van would be waiting for her in every alley, that she'd see a tattooed hand, a glinting knife, in every shadow for as long as she lived.

For a long time she sat mutely, wanting to cover herself over with the blankets and stay in this buried, candlelit chamber forever.

"Tell me it's a nightmare," she said at last,

knowing, as he gazed down into what was left of her face, what he saw. "Tell me it didn't happen—it can't be happening."

"It's not a nightmare," he replied. "It happened—and you're alive." He knelt before her, his eyes gleaming in the shadow of his hood. "Catherine, you survived. And what you endured will make you stronger, and better . . ."

She turned away, and shook her head. "I don't have your strength." She spoke from the bottom of her heart. The thought of leaving the tunnels, of even leaving this room, of having anyone, even her father, see her mutilated face, was agony to her, bitter and soul-deep humiliation, as if it were somehow a brand of punishment for something she had done. She thought, *I don't think I'd even have the courage to go out in Central Park, disguised in a hood, in the middle of the night as Vincent does.*

Her voice was small and tight. "I don't know how to do it."

"You have the strength, Catherine," said Vincent, looking across into her eyes, as if his voice, his soul, willed that strength into hers. "You *do*. I know you."

And he did. That much she knew, she understood, unquestioningly, to the very core of her soul.

After a long moment she reached forward, and lifted back the hood from his head.

He flinched, and she saw his eyes dart, as if seeking a way to run, but he stayed kneeling before her. In the candle-glow she saw how light his eyes were, like tourmaline; his hair a coarse saffron cascade over wide shoulders and halfway down his back; the short fur of his nose and muzzle like velvet the color of dust, and the straight lashes of his deep-set eyes tipped by the firelight with ginger. The cut on his forehead where the thrown reflector had struck him had scabbed over already, nearly hidden under his long hair.

Then he stood up, and reaching out, she took his hands.

"Come," he said gently. "It's time."

They ascended through the Tunnels, maze above maze, a dark and secret world. *His world*, Catherine thought, looking around her, *as surely as that golden room with its books and its statues and its poster of Einstein . . .*

Why did I never know things like this existed before?

There were tunnels cut in the living bedrock of Manhattan, gneiss and marl and veins of granite, where phosphorus gleamed dimly in the water that collected on the walls; round mains of cement or of brick that had to date back to Peter Stuyvesant's day; chasms along whose edge they moved on catwalks, the echo of their feet dying in the abyss below. In places candles had been set into niches in the rock wall; in places, battered old kerosene lanterns, or oil-burning lamps, where the footing was particularly treacherous or the way especially steep.

"Where do you get the fuel?" she asked, looking curiously up at him in the sulfurous glow. "The candles . . . there must be thousands of them . . ."

"Candles are relatively simple to make," pointed out Vincent quietly. "And the fuel . . . we have Helpers, people in the world Above. They give us what they can, like the tea I made for you. But usually they don't have much, either. Mostly we live by salvage. It's surprising, what people in your world throw away."

Like soft music, messages clanked along the bundle of pipes that ran along the wall to their right and up an ascending shaft. "Wouldn't it be easier to bleed electricity off the city lines?"

His eyes smiled. "Mouse keeps saying that . . ."

"Mouse?"

"A friend. A tinkerer . . . electricity fascinates him. He wants to install a telephone line, too. But any consistent leakage would rouse suspicion eventually, and even the smallest suspicion would be the death of our world. So many of those who live here have nowhere else to go."

Catherine remembered the afghans of Vincent's bed, made up of yarns clearly unraveled, reknotted and reknit from other garments; the blankets sewed together, like Vincent's dark, ragged mantle, from leather and scrap. As they passed through a more populated section of tunnel she looked through the raised curtain of a doorway and saw two women working at treadle sewing-machines by the light of a couple of kerosene lamps and half a dozen thick brown candles. In another place they passed lengths of obviously jury-rigged PVC pipe run through the steam pipes to heat the water within, and once, far off, Catherine thought she heard the labored thump and wheeze of a gasoline-powered donkey-engine, driving a pump. A subway rumbled by somewhere near, a reminder of the oblivious city above.

But away from the lamps and torches of habitation the tunnels were pitch-dark. Vincent guided her unerringly, holding her hand, for with a lion's face, he had a lion's night-sighted eyes. That hand, which had so frightened her once, was now only a friend's: strong enough, she sensed, to crush steel pipe, but with a light, sure touch that reminded her of the dancing classes she'd been in as a girl—the unselfconscious older boys who knew how to waltz. His palm was hairless, his touch warm in the dank tunnel chill.

Stairways and ladders of iron staples, rusted with disuse; the dim thunder of the trains; the eternal soft tapping of the pipes that ran along the tunnel ceilings and up the walls of the shafts. They passed near a door through which she glimpsed a giant chamber, a huge cavern where hundreds of pipes ran together. A little balding man was tapping on them with a wrench, bending his shiny head to listen to a staccato chaos of replies in the glow of half a dozen candles stuck in old Night Train bottles. He looked up as Vincent passed, and waved a greeting with his wrench. Three children clothed in patches and leather ran by, calling Vincent's name happily. To them, Catherine realized, as to her now, he was not a monster but a friend, someone trusted and known.

In this world he was safe.

And she too, she thought with sudden surprise. There had been no lock on the door of Vincent's room, and most of these chambers had only curtains for doors. The low arched corridors, filled with shadow, held for her not a scrap of fear. Not fear of the men in the van, the man with the knife—not fear of being seen. Like Vincent, she walked with her ruined face uncovered, and it occurred to her belatedly that the glances those children had given her had been only curiosity at a stranger, not at a deformed freak.

They crossed a chasm spanned by arched bridges built by God knew whom; traversed a softly hissing steam tunnel, warm from the pipes along its walls; climbed another ladder. In what looked like the tube of a long-abandoned subway-line Vincent sprang lightly across a steam-filled crevasse in the half-dark, held out his hand to her. "You can do it," his deep voice urged from the dark.

And, just touching his fingers to leap, she could.

Then a stair of pierced iron rungs, a long twisting spiral, level upon level, upwards from the world Below.

In a round-walled corridor their feet plashed softly through standing water. She was tired now, unaccustomed to walking and weak from her convalescence. His arm in its quilted sleeve was strong and steadying, the familiar Tunnel smells of candle smoke and earth comforting in the folds of his coat. Another short climb, then a tiny doorway roughly hewed in cement and bricks, concealed in some dark cement room filled with moldering boxes and the smell of mildew and mice. At the far end another doorway, a short hall, iron staples leading up to a grilled opening through which bluish light poured down in a misty column.

Vincent said simply, "This is where you go out."

"Where are we?"

"The basement of your apartment building."

The prosaic conclusion to the climb from the world Below made her laugh; when he had asked her address earlier, she had supposed it was only curiosity. But of course Vincent, who had roved the Tunnels all his life, would have been able to pinpoint the place from the underside as easily as she'd be able to guess at the location of an address on Third Avenue.

Silence lay between them. They stood, fingers touching, in the semi-dark, before the door that led back to her world—the door she knew would close behind her when she passed through it, concealing the secret world of the Tunnels in its protective darkness once again.

On the other side of that door, she understood, she would have to go up to her apartment, face the astounded stare, the humiliating pity, of the elevator man, the building concierge, whoever else happened to be in the lobby. Would have to telephone her father . . . would have to endure stares, pity, questioning by the police, explanation after explanation, hearing everyone gasp and say "Oh, my God!" and look the other way.

But for these last few minutes, on this side of the door, she was utterly safe.

Safe with Vincent.

She looked up at his face, and by the wan reflection of that column of infalling light saw in his eyes, as well as care and concern for her, a deep and aching grief.

His care—his voice when she'd wake in the nights, his undemanding gentleness—were the only reasons, she realized, that she was able now to go through that door and confront the horrors she knew she'd have to face on the other side. He believed in her strength to do it, and she had come, insensibly, to trust that what he said was true; this as well as the rest, whether she felt it in her exhausted heart or not.

He had, in fact, saved her life: physically in the park, which was already like some murky nightmare, attenuated by time. And in a deeper sense, he had saved her capacity for life.

And this was going to be the last she'd see of him, this beautiful lion in the patched coat, this strong and gentle friend.

Her fingers closed around the pawlike hand. "Your secret is safe with me, you know," she said, looking up into his face. "I'd never betray your trust."

He shook his head. "I know." His voice, always so quiet, was barely audible, as if he held some great emotion desperately in check. "I knew that from the beginning, when *you* trusted *me*."

Hesitantly, she took a step toward him, then reached out, and put her arms around his body. She felt a shiver pass through him at her touch, the tension and the ragged release of his breath. Then his arm closed around her, holding her to him, feeling beneath the worn wool and leather of his coat the hard muscle of his chest, the rough silk mane mingling with her hair.

"What can I say to you?" she whispered. In his arms, her head pressed to his broad shoulder, she was safe, and for a time she wanted nothing more than to remain there forever.

Footsteps echoed sharply in the basement above. They were standing together where the diffuse light came through the door. When Vincent ducked back with his reflex caution, shunning the light and the world above, Catherine slipped back with him into the shadows. For a moment she stood, listening, recognizing the soft Virginia accent of the building supervisor, speaking to one of his assistants. Odd that his would be the first voice she heard on her return . . .

The footsteps faded, the voices died. She turned back . . .

Vincent was gone.

"Vincent!" She took a few steps back into that black room, but knew she'd never find him—

probably never even find the opening through which they'd come. "Vincent . . ."

There was no reply.

She stood for a long moment in the dark, feeling wholly bereft. Somewhere in the building the steam pipes made a soft clanking, reminding her of the heartbeat of the world Below.

For a brief moment she thought that she would sooner walk across the lobby naked than with her face as it was. The comparison was apt, she realized—more apt than she had known before. She had always worn her beauty, her careful and fashionable perfection, like a garment, to protect and conceal the person underneath.

And now it was gone.

The next few days, she knew, were going to be more awful than she cared to think about.

But she'd get through them. They were, after all, only days.

She gathered her coat closer about her, drew up the plum-colored scarf to cover her head—to hide what the men in the van had left her of her face.

With firm strides, her high heels sounding softly on the damp concrete, she stepped through the door into her own world again.

From the darkness of the tunnel entrance Vincent watched her as she stepped over the low brick doorsill, walked down the short corridor away from him, until she stepped into the white light pouring down from above. Then like a curtain the light closed around her, and she was gone.

Five

Dialing the telephone for that first call was perhaps the most difficult thing she had ever done.

"Jenny?"

"*CATHY?*"

"Yes . . ." She couldn't say anything else. Her throat seemed to close—tears, disorientation such as she had never known in her life, an agony of dread. The shocked stare of the elevator man, the horrified silence of the concierge, were raw on her soul like whip cuts. She'd gotten across the lobby, up the elevator, down her own hallway to 21B somehow. She still didn't know how.

Jenny, as always, was practical, something one had to be if one dealt with authors all day. "Where are you?"

"I'm at home . . . " whispered Catherine, the straightforward request for information freeing the strangling tension in her throat. "At my apartment . . . I just got back." *God, what a phrase,* she thought distractedly, *it sounds like I just got off the boat from the Bahamas.*

"Are you all right?"

"Not really. Can you come over, please . . . ?"

"I'll be there in five minutes. Should I bring anything?"

"No." She could hear the logjam of questions in her friend's brief pause, and fought to keep from bursting into tears, from stammering out an explanation, an apology in advance. "Just please come."

"Be right there."

Catherine hung up. Her hand around the receiver of the pale-pink phone—an impulsive gift from her father, who had a habit of buying her presents he thought she'd like, everything from Rolex watches all the way up to the eighteenth-century secretaire in the corner—was shaking and clammy with sweat, and she felt as if she were about to faint.

It was the walk up from the Tunnels, she told herself, trying to breathe. She was physically exhausted, she'd only been on her feet for a few days . . . That was what accounted for the nausea, the terror, the frenzied desire to weep and not stop weeping.

Vincent . . .

Don't be silly, she told herself. There was of course no way Vincent could have accompanied her past the hidden door in the sub-basement, no way he could let himself be seen in the daylight world. She had to do this by herself.

Of course she was strong enough. He'd said so. He knew her.

A bus went by on Central Park West, roaring like an airplane even at the distance of four stories; taxis honked, the drone of traffic shuddered noisily in the soft lapis air. After the silence of the Tunnels the noise was hideous, distracting, bludgeoning her like a hammer. She reached for the telephone again, and drew her hand back, unable for the moment to touch it. *Not just yet . . .*

Her eyes went to the clock. Eight-thirty. It was over a week, she realized, since she'd seen a clock, or known what time it was. Below the ground it was always night. Beyond the latticed French doors which let out onto the terrace the eastern air was deepening from translucence into final darkness. Beyond Central Park she could see the lights of Fifth Avenue, snagged like jewels in the dark frieze of branches.

It had been over a week since she'd used a telephone.

Missing for over a week, my God, Dad . . .

But she couldn't touch the phone. She squeezed her hands together to keep them from shaking, moved to press them over her mouth, a gesture to keep her from bursting into tears. But her fingers came in contact with the sutured wreck of her lip and she jerked them violently away.

I can't go into hysterics now, she told herself desperately. *If I do I won't be able to stop. I can't be crying when I call Dad. I can't . . .*

Guilt at not having called him first thing made her almost physically ill. She had known it ought to be her first impulse, her first call, but she had sat in front of the phone for nearly thirty minutes in the slowly gathering gloom, unable to face the thought of his reaction. It would be caring, it would be loving, it would be stricken with horror and pain for her sake.

And in the end, she'd called Jenny.

Of the group of girls she had known at Radcliffe, Jenny Aronsen was the only one with whom she had remained close, or as close as their wildly

57

divergent social lives had let them in the ensuing years. Nancy Hoyt—Nancy Tucker, now—her closest friend of those days, was married now and living in Westport, Connecticut. For a moment her hand flinched toward the phone again at the thought of her friend, but she drew it back. There was nothing Nancy could do, and calling her now would only frighten and upset her . . . Besides, Catherine sincerely doubted her own ability to speak more than two sentences without bursting into tears.

She had to call her father. She knew she had to call her father.

Her hands was shaking too badly to dial. Reaching out, she switched on the sandstone-colored lamp on the table beside her. The small pool of golden brightness seemed to plunge the rest of the graceful little room into deeper shade, and, suddenly scared, Catherine got to her feet and went to turn on the torchère, the reading lamp by the secretaire. The door of the bedroom suddenly seemed to gape at her, a black and sinister mouth. *My God, somebody could have been hiding there all this time . . .*

Every light in the place was burning when Jenny arrived. Her knock nearly startled Catherine out of her skin, but for a moment Catherine sat frozen in the chair by the telephone where she had collapsed again. She wondered what on earth had possessed her to turn the lights on. It was darkness she wanted, shadow to hide her face, the darkness of refuge, of sanctuary. Like Vincent, she wanted to remain hooded, hidden away.

But of course, she realized, Vincent walked hooded in darkness only for the sake of safety, not out of any sort of shame in the way he looked.

"Cathy?" Through the door Jenny sounded worried and scared. Catherine debated for a moment going up to the door and explaining what had happened through the panels, breaking it to her easy so she wouldn't stare, wouldn't gasp, wouldn't . . . (*Wouldn't remind her how hideous she had become?*)

She got to her feet, and without a word opened the door.

Jenny stopped short on the threshhold for one second, her brown eyes flaring with shock; then she stepped inside and caught Catherine in a fierce, welcoming hug.

Jenny offered to call her father. "Look, if you're worried about how he'll take it, don't put yourself through it," said the dark-haired girl in her low, sensible voice. She wore jeans over a lavender leotard, having just gotten back from the gym when Catherine called, and still managed to look like a fashion model, something Jenny was good at—at barely five-feet-two, Catherine had always good-naturedly envied her graceful height.

Catherine shook her head. "No. I'll do it." She didn't want to say that she couldn't let her father think he hadn't been the first one she'd called. Whatever Jenny thought—and ever since college her friend had been an observer of a great deal of her loving, but oddly awkward relationship with her father—she kept to herself, and silently Catherine thanked her for it as she dialed the telephone. It was easier with someone else there.

During the conversation itself, Jenny went into the sleek honey-and-white kitchen and made tea.

"Daddy?"

There was shocked, horrified silence on the other end of the line. Then, as if he had only regained his breath, the words poured in a rush. "*Cathy*! Oh, my God, where have you been? What happened?"

"Daddy, listen—"

"Darling, are you all right? Where are you? I'll come and get you . . ."

"Daddy, I'm home." *That stupid phrase again*. She swallowed hard. "Daddy, listen . . ."

"The police have been looking for you all over the state!"

"Daddy, *please*." The desperation in her voice silenced him. She made herself frame the next words with agonizing effort. "Daddy, I . . . I was mugged. I'm . . . I'm more or less all right."

"Oh, my darling . . ."

Don't start, please don't start, this is hard enough without you coming to pieces.

"I'll be right over there. Have you called the police? Does Tom know?"

"Don't you dare call Tom!" The words came out in a gasp that shocked her. "Please," she added, trying to mollify him, aghast that she'd shouted at him, not quite knowing why she didn't want Tom to see her this way but knowing to the bottom of her soul that she did not. "Please. I was . . . I was hurt, cut with a knife." *Don't gasp. Don't say 'Oh, my God.'*

"Oh, my God."

She closed her eyes, unable to go on, listening to his horrified, half-incoherent stammerings. "Oh, my darling, my baby . . . I'll be right over. Shall I bring a doctor?"

"No," she said, her voice shaking. "I just . . . I'm all right."

"I'll be there. I'll be there right away, my darling."

She set the phone down, weak with a guilt that she was hard-put to define, though it overwhelmed her. Since her mother's death she'd been responsible for his happiness. Though what had happened to her had been in no way her fault (*had it?*), she felt that somehow she had let him down, as she had let him down, daily, for two years by not being the best corporate lawyer in New York.

Tears burned her eyes. She bowed her head, and felt again, as she pressed her hands to her face, the welted horror of sutures and scars.

Jenny's strong, slim hands gripped her neck and shoulders comfortingly, and lowering her head, Catherine cried.

Her father brought the police. From where she sat on the couch, Catherine looked up when Jenny went to answer that hurried, anxious knock on the door, and saw her friend freeze into shocked immobility as she opened it. Jenny looked like she would have spoken, had she been able to find anything to say, but the next instant Charles Chandler came hurrying into the room with a burly white-haired captain of detectives on his heels, a uniformed officer and a police photographer in their wake.

Of course her father would have brought the police, thought Catherine, closing her eyes despairingly. "Oh, my darling," he whispered, staring at her, horror and grief and guilt—guilt that he had been unable to protect her—naked upon his face. Of course his first thought would have been to phone the police, not even thinking that they would insist on coming with him to question her. Not thinking that she might not welcome being seen by three total strangers, that there might have been things she couldn't or wouldn't tell him on the phone. He had thought only of protecting her, avenging her, doing what he knew to be best for her because it was what he had always done.

For a moment he stared at her, with her marked face now swollen and red from weeping as well, and she thought that he too was perilously near to tears.

"Oh, Cathy . . ."

She held out her arms to him, realizing suddenly that, in an odd way, what he needed of her was her strength, her forgiveness. His face was horribly haggard, purple smudges of sleeplessness and stress marking his eyes; he looked visibly thinner than he had ten days ago (*Ten days?! Had it really only been that?*), sitting in his comfortable, oak-paneled office, asking worriedly, "What's up with you?" back in that other lifetime when her only problem had been what she was going to wear to Tom's party that night.

When he hugged her, desperately tight, she gritted her teeth and didn't mention the broken rib, not wanting him to feel worse than he did.

But inside she felt emptied, as if she had called his name in darkness, and he had not replied.

"Cathy," he stammered, as he gently released her, sat on the couch at her side, "this is Captain John Hermann of the NYPD." The big burly man in the rumpled raincoat nodded to her, looking at her face and then surreptitiously away. "He's working on your case. They'll get the men who did this, darling, they'll make them pay."

Pay for what? thought Catherine blankly, exhausted and wanting only to sleep, feeling naked before those strangers' stares.

"He just wants to ask you a few questions."

"No." She flinched back and shook her head desperately, her dirty hair slapping against her cheeks, then turned away, fighting a sudden, racking sob. *Dammit, I will NOT burst into tears in front of them.*

She had promised Vincent. She owed them. They had given her her life; the least she could give was her silence

"If you can give us a description of the men who did this, it would help," said Hermann, pulling a report-book from his raincoat pocket. "You've been missing for the last ten days, Miss Chandler. We were waiting for a ransom note."

"Please, I don't want to talk about it."

"Were they keeping you prisoner?"

"*No,*" she stammered. "No, I wasn't . . . I just . . . I can't talk about it now." She raised her head, and a flashbulb went off in her eyes, making her wince.

"Just for the records, miss," explained the police photographer, as if that would excuse preserving for posterity the hideous remains of her face. Standing framed in the lighted doorway to the kitchen, Jenny pressed her lips hard together and said nothing, but her dark eyes smoldered with anger for her friend.

"Really, any help you can give us, Miss Chandler . . ."

"My darling, we've been so worried about you." Her father was collecting himself a little, but from the corner of her eye she could still see the shock on his face, the sickened guilt.

"I can't." She swallowed hard. "I can't talk about it now. I'll . . . later . . ."

Hermann looked put out, his lips twisting with annoyance that he couldn't make out his report tonight, and Catherine felt the hopeless, ludicrous sense of having let him down, as well. She knew she should tell him something, try to fumble together some story, some train of events that would sound convincing but not lead anyone to the Tunnels, to Vincent.

But her mind was a blank. Her thoughts, raw with misery and exhaustion, chased one another around and always came looping back to the fact that all she wanted to do was lie down, all she wanted was for them to go away, to stop staring at her, to stop that almost-audible whisper of speculation in their minds about what had happened, what they'd done to her.

Go away! she thought bitterly. *Please, please, PLEASE go away . . .*

It seemed like forever until they left. Jenny, practical as ever, vanished during the proceedings and returned just as the police were leaving, a bag of groceries in her arms. Of course after ten days there was nothing in the refrigerator worth eating, not that Catherine ever cooked much for herself anyway. Generally she ate out, with Tom, or her father, or one of the other men she occasionally dated. Lying on her bed, still in that rumpled, mended black party dress, she could hear Jenny in the other room talking softly with her father, convincing him tactfully that probably the best thing he could do was leave her to get some sleep.

"I'll stay here with her, in case she needs anything in the night," the tall girl said, her soft voice almost inaudible over the muffled gurgle of water from the bathroom where she'd turned on the water for a bath. It was nearly midnight. Catherine felt like she'd been walking for days, stumbling through this endless hell of stares, whispers, people around her . . .

The Tunnels—Vincent—the strange, dim world Below, seemed endlessly far away.

"Cathy?"

She looked up, to see her father framed in the doorway.

The room was dim. With others there the darkness did not frighten her as it had done, and she felt better, more secure, as she felt instinctively Vincent did in shadow. Light filtering through the French doors outlined the shapes of the furnishings, cool modern accented with an occasional eighteenth-century antique, and reduced the two large, sandstone-colored abstract paintings to the lights and darks of their compositions. Her father was a bulk of shadow, a gleam of silver on white hair. His voice was hesitant, helpless.

"Thank you," she whispered, knowing he still needed reassurance, still needed—what? To know she forgave him for not having rescued her? For not having been a good enough father to have prevented all this? "Thank you for coming . . . for being there." Never mind that his efforts in that direction had involved bringing in strangers to stare at her, to question her, to ask her about being carved up, beaten, thrown out of a van to die. That was not what he needed to hear.

How strange, she thought, to have found the strength, not only for herself, but for him.

Later, bathed, hair washed, the satin of her nightgown soft on her skin, she lay in the cool familiarity of her own bed, listening to the sounds of New York. Rosy light burned in the living room and would burn all night, reassuring should she wake in the dark, but somehow, after her first fears that somehow the men in the van had followed her, dark did not really bother her anymore. Odd, because as a child she had always feared it; even as an adult she had frequently slept with a night light.

But she had known the dark of blindness, and of the Tunnels; no darkness up here could compare with either of those.

Turned down low, the murmur of the TV set in the living room was still vaguely intrusive where Jenny sat reading whatever portion of the editorial slush-pile was occupying her tote-bag that week, leaving her to her sleep—unfamiliar after the silence below the ground. Down on Central Park West the throb of New York traffic rumbled endless, alien and vaguely threatening. Her own bed felt odd, neat and rather prim after the yielding tangle of Vincent's quilts and pillows and furs.

She found she missed the soft tapping of the pipes, the deep and wonderful variations of Vincent's voice as he read aloud to her the manifold adventures of Pip and Estella, Herbert and Clara. She wondered where Vincent was, and what he was doing; whether he was walking, as he had been that night, concealed in his drawn-up hood of leather and patches, in the wet grass and concealing shadows of the park.

And so wondering, she slept.

Six

CATHERINE had always hated hospitals. Even the sunny Children's Ward of the New York Medical Center where she'd had her tonsils out at age seven had made her nervous, with its antiseptic smells and the sense of hidden things going on behind bright facades. One of her clearest memories, isolated and out of context, was waking in the dark ward in the middle of the night and hearing the voice of some other child, she didn't know who or where, screaming frantically on the other side of a wall.

But mostly it was the memory of coming into a stark white room and seeing her mother, thin and chalky and horribly unfamiliar, lying propped on a bed with tubes in her arms and mouth and nose. The only thing left of the warm and loving presence Catherine remembered had been the wheat-blonde hair, lighter than her own and wavy, spread out over the pillow, and the sunrise beauty of her smile. She hadn't wanted to look at her, or to touch the soft hand with the tube taped to the back of it where it protruded from the big vein, but she had, though she didn't remember what either of them had said. Then a nurse had taken her out to wait in the hall. She was only ten, and to this day she remembered the red plaid dress she'd been wearing, the black velvet jacket. There had been an old man with no legs out there, being pushed in a wheelchair down to the toilets at the end of the hall. Catherine had closed her eyes and stood pressed to the wall, wanting not to see any of it, wanting not to be there, wanting none of this to be real. After forever her father had come out, and took her home, not speaking. She'd never seen her mother again.

"Cathy," said Dr. Sanderly in his kindest voice, "I want you to start counting from ten, backwards."

They'd already given her Valium in her room. It had let her lie on the gurney in pre-op with equanimity while they drew circles in antiseptic blue pen around the scars on her face. *Like those horrible old 'forties cartoons,* she thought dreamily, *where the fairy-tale headsman whips out a pen and draws a dotted line on the prospective victim's neck before a beheading. My God, what a gruesome thing to show to kids!* She couldn't remember what cartoon it had been—Betty Boop? Heckle and Jeckle? Trying to identify the scene distracted her from the quaky dread in her stomach, the hideous smells of the room around her—antiseptic, ether, rubbing alcohol—and kept at bay the muted chatter of anesthesiologists and O.R. nurses, and the soft, sinister clinking of their little tools.

Through the plastic mask covering mouth and nose she mumbled "Ten . . . nine . . . eight . . ." smelled and heard the gas hissing.

She made it down to four.

Then she was in the corridor outside her father's

office, late for work again—by the sunlight falling through the windows in the reception area she knew it was two or three in the afternoon. She was stumbling, clutching the torn rags of the black party dress around her, her face the scarred nightmare she had first seen in the distorted reflection of the silver bowl. She had to reach her father, had to tell him she was back. (*But you phoned him . . . You DID phone him, though he should have been the first, and anyway he didn't know he wasn't the first.*)

The office door popped open and Charles Chandler looked out, immaculately barbered as ever, gray-suited, silver-haired, and perfect as he always was. "Cathy!" he exclaimed with a cheerful smile. "So you finally got in! We were all guessing where you went—was it Jamaica? Nassau?"

She stood, holding the torn dress around her, staring at him wordlessly, unable to speak, knowing he barely saw her because he didn't want to see her—didn't want to see pain and ugliness, didn't want to see what had befallen her because it reflected badly on him as a parent.

"Let's get some people together," he was saying, a favorite expression of his, "we'll have a party. My club, shall it be? Whom shall we invite?"

No, she thought numbly, still unable to speak. *It wasn't like this. He didn't flinch much when he saw me—didn't look away for more than a second or so—he was caring, loving . . . He held me, rocked me like a child in his arms.*

"I have to run." He smiled, still not looking at her. "I'm in a board meeting." From his coat he pulled a thick wad of bills. "Here . . . buy yourself a new dress—will this be enough?" (*Or was it, "Buy yourself a new face"?*) He pressed the money into her hands. "Take some more, here."

He closed the door in her face. She stood in the hall, her hands full of money; she had nowhere to put it.

"Dad," she whispered, to the shut oak panels. "Dad . . ."

(After the police had gone he had talked plastic surgery; he had said, "Best in the field"; he had said, "They're looking for the men who did this—they won't get away." "Darling, darling, oh my baby," in that hurt, shocked, frightened voice. He hadn't asked if she were still afraid; he hadn't said, "When you're ready." He had asked, instead, why she hadn't told Captain Hermann where she'd been, what had happened to her—why she wouldn't tell him. He hadn't said, "Is there anything you need?" He had always known what she needed, gotten it for her before she'd thought to ask. *We'll wipe up the spill, honey, and I'll buy you some more milk, and it'll never have happened.*)

She stumbled down the corridor, endlessly long as the corridors in dreams always are, her hands full of money that fell on the thick beige carpet behind her like staggering footprints. Clerks, secretaries, junior staff brushed past her, beautifully dressed—why had she never noticed how careful everyone in the office was about what they wore? How uptown they all were?—and smiling at her in the way they did when she'd breeze in late and they didn't say anything because she was Charles Chandler's daughter.

"You have a nice vacation?" asked one, not looking—after the first surreptitious glance—at her face. "You look—uh—great."

"Where'd you go?"

"We missed you."

And like froth in the wake of a passing ship the

whispers curled back: "Pathetic, isn't it?" "How'd it happen?" "She used to be so pretty." "Was she raped as well?"

She began to run. She wasn't in a hallway at all, but in an alley. Headlights switched on behind her, the low wet growl of tires on pavement, the black bulk of a van blocking the street lamps beyond. Her high heels twisted and wobbled on the broken asphalt, she couldn't run fast enough . . . panic mounted in her, thrashing like an unvoiced scream as she tried to flee and found herself moving in a hideous slow-motion, while the van grew larger and larger behind. The doors clanged open—a man said something to her, she didn't remember what—a knife flashed in a tattooed hand—she was flung down . . .

She sprawled on the floor, but it was not the bare metal floor of the van. Instead it was the plush burnt-orange carpeting of the ballroom of the Barron Hotel—why was she able to remember it was orange?—and she twisted up onto her elbows, surrounded by a sea of legs. Soft Muzak played an infinitely watered-down version of "Eine Kleine Nachtmusik"; laughter floated detached around her like a sparkling fog; glasses clinked against caviar spoons and a waiter said something in Spanish. She heard Tom's voice and half rolled over to look. He was standing with a beautiful blonde woman in a lamé pantsuit, drink in hand; he did not see her under their feet, in her ripped and dirty dress, her mauled face and unwashed hair.

"I feel sorry for her," Tom was saying in a tone she remembered, the half-protesting, half-excusing tone he'd use for statements like "Well, of course the homeless need shelter of some kind." "But what can you do? Life goes on."

That was an expression he was fond of, usually accompanied, as it was now, by a boyish twinkle and a philosophical little shrug which completely dismissed whatever he was talking about. The woman nodded her immaculately coifed head.

"She was an interesting girl, I thought she had a lot of promise. But she turned out to be a complete loser." He put his arm around the woman's waist, and a man Catherine recognized as the city building commissioner made a noise of assent.

Behind her, someone started to laugh.

Catherine looked around, her breath catching in a little sob. *It's not my fault*, she wanted to cry, but her disfigured lips would make no sound. *What happened to me wasn't my fault*. But her fault or not, she was no longer beautiful, no longer perfect . . . no longer acceptable. Only herself.

Someone else giggled. A woman pointed a mauve fingernail, another member of the Building Commission didn't quite manage to hide his grin behind a handful of martini. The laughter swelled, men and women, some of them trying to be polite out of pity and turning away or covering their mouths, others snickering openly, pointing to the ragged and ugly girl sprawled on the floor. She felt weak, as she had when she'd first wakened—somehow she knew she couldn't stand, and that if she wanted to escape she'd have to do so on her hands and knees. Trapped, in agony, all her old defenses gone, she looked around for some way out . . .

. . . and saw Vincent, strong and shaggy and beautiful, standing in the doorway at the back of the crowd. The shadows of his hood hid his strange unhuman face, but there was sorrow, and empathy, and caring in his eyes.

And slowly, she got to her feet.

In the solitude of his chamber Vincent sat, his head bowed over his folded hands. A volume of Shakespeare lay open in front of him, but for the last half hour he had not been reading. Candles burned all around him, the eternal half-night of Below, though he knew it was midmorning. In a short time he'd have to go, with a troop of the children, to meet one of the Helpers who'd promised to send down food from above—a long walk up to Harlem, through passages far beyond the range of habitation and lights.

But now, alone and in silence, he could feel the silent horrors of Catherine's dreams.

He knew they were hers, as he had known, these last few days, that the distant whisper of emotions that came to him like the far-off clankings of the pipes emanated from her heart. They were completely inchoate, for the brain, as Father liked to point out, has no nerve endings: it is the body that feels pain and joy. As he had climbed down the iron rungs from the sub-basement of Catherine's apartment building on Central Park West, as he had moved through the lightless steam tunnels, across the Chasm and down the Long Stair, he had felt her distress and her fear. He had supposed then that it had been the effect of being with her, of knowing what she'd have to go through to return to her world.

Only later it had come to him that the link between them, forged in this room as he'd watched over her while she slept, had not been severed.

Earlier today he had felt her apprehension, the

braced dread of doing something—what?—that she knew she'd have to do. And now, suddenly, this torrent of cloudy hurt and apprehension that he somehow knew to be dreams, backed by the drug-muffled whisper of pain.

Closing his eyes, he whispered, "I'm with you, Catherine," though he knew she couldn't hear.

In a sense he knew he would always be with her, and the knowledge was a mingling of joy and despair. For in the cellar, when she had stepped into his arms, he had come to understand that he loved her, and it was the realization of all that such a love implied, as much as the sound of footsteps from Above, which had driven him away.

Vincent loved many people: his father, his friends in the Tunnels, the children he taught and guarded. But no one whose simple touch went through him like electricity, no one for whom he felt this terrible longing; no one to whom he felt linked, as he did with this beautiful woman who had visited his world so briefly, and then returned—as return she must—to the city of daylight Above.

And there was nothing he could do.

He opened his eyes, and looked at his hand, spread out before him in the candlelight. *If I profane by my unworthiest hand . . .* Romeo had said, reaching to touch the fingers of the woman he had known, when first he saw her, to be the other half of his soul. Even the comparison was a kind of ironic jest. He remembered how Catherine's fingers had first touched his, then jerked away with a cry. Turning his hand over, he examined, dispassionately, the long reddish hair and the powerful, knotted fingers, the wax-yellow claws veined with purplish brown. Truly a monster's hand.

There was nothing he could do about that either. Not even, apparently, forget.

He had become acutely aware of love and lovers, in these last few days. Books he had read again with a different awareness, as if subtexts written in colors to which he had been blind had risen suddenly to the surface like invisible ink. The extraordinary passion of Yuri Zhivago for Lara Antipova, of the Chevalier des Grieux for Manon Lescaut, made perfect sense to him now, and though he had always known that his father cared deeply for the gentle midwife Mary, he saw when those two worked together now an entirely different world in the casual contact of eye and hand.

Later, as he came down the rough wooden steps to the junction near the pipe-chamber where the little Harlem party was to meet him, he was aware of the oldest of the girls—a plain and skinny sixteen-year-old named Kirsten Ho—standing apart from the others, in quiet talk with Luke, one of the community's young men.

Only a few of the close-knit family of those who dwelled Below had been actually born there. Pascal, who played the endless tapped relays on the master-pipes—a boy named Devin, with whom Vincent had grown up like a brother, before Devin had left to seek his own dreams above the ground. For the most part those who comprised the community had found their way down from Above, either as adults, like Father and old Elizabeth who dwelled in the Painted Tunnels, or as children. Luke was one of these, a chunky young man who had been adopted into the Undercity at the age of six or seven when his only remaining family, an aunt and a Helper herself, had died of cancer. Red-haired, clumsy, and a little simple, he was tireless and eternally good-hearted. He would be nineteen or twenty now, Vincent guessed, watching his square, earnest face in the bar of light that fell through the pipe-room door as he talked to Ho.

"I'm not trying to push you," Luke was saying in a quiet voice. "You know I don't mean now. But I had to tell you . . . I had to talk to you."

And the girl Ho sighed, and turned her face away, the wide rectangle of her lips pressing tight with indecision and unhappiness. Luke caught her shoulders impatiently, forcing her to turn back to him, demanding that she hear what he had to say.

But whatever that was was drowned as the children crowded up around Vincent, each volunteering his or her abilities to guide the expedition to Harlem unerringly—a long trek, by Tunnel standards, and a complicated one. "Kipper guides us as far as the Catacombs," Vincent ruled, judging the boy enough of an expert in that particular stretch not to disgrace himself by having to ask for help, and the dark-haired urchin beamed with pride. The others shouldered the crates and baskets—a change in the fashions of knickknackery had put a large number of baskets of various sizes into the purlieu of the tunnel dwellers—and Ho, walking swiftly across the dim, cement-floored chamber, caught up the drag-rope of a light, three-wheeled cart.

"I'll help with that," volunteered Luke, hurrying after her, and she turned on him with a kind of despairing impatience, dark eyes snapping.

"We would appreciate your help, Luke," interjected Vincent quietly, before the girl could speak. "But Winslow asked me to tell you he needs help with the new gate up under the Stuyvesant Square entrance. Would you be free for that?"

"Uh . . ." Luke stepped back from Ho's seething gaze. "Sure. I'll, uh, see you later."

And he hurried off, his feet splashing softly in the trickle of groundwater that covered the cement.

"Why does he have to do that?" sighed Ho, falling behind the children to walk in step with Vincent, who padded softly in the rear. "Why can't he just let me alone?" Her narrow face, in which Negroid and Vietnamese features blended under a cap of fine, tightly braided hair, still had a closed look to it, uncertain but giving nothing away.

Why indeed? thought Vincent, who liked the girl's scrappy toughness and had a good deal of sympathy for Luke's desire to know where matters stood. "Perhaps because he's known you half his life?"

She sniffed, such matters cutting little ice at sixteen.

Ahead of them, the beam of Kipper's lantern glanced across a grillwork of rusty iron bars, formed to fit the circular shape of the old main through which they walked. Vincent came forward and unlocked the padlock on the heavy door, put his shoulder to it and pushed it open, the metal making a faint protesting groan. Periodically Mouse would tinker together automated mechanisms for one or another of the gates, but in addition to Mouse's artistic objections to doing anything the same way twice, parts for such devices were hard to come by, and most of the gates and doors Below were manually operated still.

They ascended a long, makeshift ramp constructed of scrap lumber and plywood, the gleam of the lanterns throwing jogging shadows across the concrete curves of the Tunnel walls and glinting crookedly on runnels and patches of seep-water on the floor. In places grilles of old chick-enwire and chain-link fencing covered vents that led to deeper tunnels; in others, these holes gaped open like dry black mouths. Here and there warning signs were posted. The children walked in silence, counting off entrances and branches, as Vincent and the others taught them to do. Out here, far from the inhabited portions of the Tunnels, it was perilously easy to get lost.

Along the curved wall to their left the pipes clanked in a rapid-fire whisper, and somewhere below, the trickle of water echoed in the dark. Over their heads the Lexington Avenue Express rushed by like unseen wind.

"Is there someone else?" asked Vincent after a long silence, feeling the pent desperation, the anger of the girl beside him, loud as the beating of wings against bars.

"I'd like there to be," sighed Ho. "I mean, he'd understand that. But it's just—I don't *like* him. I mean, I like him, but I don't *like* him. Not like he wants me to. And he won't leave me alone."

Vincent sighed, remembering the anxious adora-tion in Luke's eyes. There were worse things, he supposed, than loving someone you would never see again; and from that he tried to take what comfort he could. Catherine had returned to her world—for him, there was and always would be only this.

"Vincent?"

For one second, before she tried to open her eyes, Catherine imagined that she was back in the safety of Vincent's chamber. Her first awareness was of the dull ache of her face beneath its bandages, a surge of déjà vu before the smell of disinfectant and surgical dressing—almost masked by the cloying scent of flowers—and the far-off throb of traffic far below told her where she had to be.

"Cathy?" a man's voice said. "It's Dr. Sanderly."

Her mind, sodden with anesthetic and phenobarbital, groped at the name, and she remembered her father's voice saying, "Sanderly's the best cosmetic surgeon in the business. I'll have him flown in from L.A. Don't worry. Don't worry about a thing."

(*Buy yourself a new dress*, whispered a voice from some covered pit in the bottom of her mind. *Buy yourself a new face*.)

She pushed the thoughts away. It wasn't his fault that his first instinct was to make everything look like nothing had happened. *If it looks okay, it is okay, right*? He would be a bad parent if it wasn't. Like Vincent, he was what he was. What he gave her was everything he could.

Her mouth felt like she'd rented it cheap and they hadn't got the fit right. "I'm in the hospital?"

"Yes . . . and you're going to be fine."

He was standing beside her bed—she could smell his aftershave. Aramis. Tom wore it, too. She remembered him now from pre-op, drawing dreadful little circles on her face with a felt-tip pen. The smell of flowers lay thick in the dry, air-conditioned chill. Roses and . . . what? Something else. How absurd of them to have sent her flowers she wouldn't be able to see for days.

She wondered what time it was. Her father

undoubtedly had a meeting with one of his big accounts, but would come as soon as he was free.

"You must've gone through a terrible ordeal," Sanderly continued, stepping close to pat her hand. "But whatever happened is behind you now—completely behind you."

Meaning, she supposed, she looked—or would look, when the stitches healed and the swelling went down—just like she had before. Weary to her bones, queasy with the aftermath of the ether and groggy from the painkillers, she could not care, could not feel anything but a tiredness worlds deep. It was behind her now: the look of shocked and sickened horror on her father's face when he'd stepped through the apartment door and seen her sitting on the couch; the way the elevator man in her building had stared and gasped "*Miss Chandler!*"; the nurses in the hospital who had stared when they'd come in, she bundled up like Vincent in a hooded cloak, and then had quickly looked away. All those awful little humiliations which, thank God—thanks to her father's money—she was not going to have to put up with for the rest of her life, or for as many years as it would have taken her to collect the money to have the scars erased.

But she would never forget how it had felt.

Behind her, too, the soft tapping of the pipes in the Tunnels; the strength of Vincent's arms around her as she'd pressed her ruined cheek to his shoulder; the bronze and velvet of his voice.

And ahead . . .

What?

Sanderly went on, professional and kind. "If there's anything you want to tell me, or talk to me about . . . anything I can do, just let me know."

He was already crossing the room away from her and she heard his hand on the doorknob. He had, she supposed, other patients to see.

But his intention was kind, and she made herself say, "Thanks," though it hurt her mouth.

She heard the door open and shut, leaving her alone with her flowers.

Wistfully, she added to no one in particular, "You could read me the last chapter of *Great Expectations*."

Seven

Eight months passed. Life, as Tom Gunther liked to observe, went on, Above and Below.

For Catherine it was a time of change.

Her father offered to send her anywhere—Paris, the Bahamas, Cancun. She had thanked him, her voice smiling though her face couldn't yet, clasping his hands where he sat on the stiff plastic chair beside her hospital bed, and had opted to remain in New York.

That was the day the detectives had been in. Captain Hermann, still is his rumpled raincoat, had asked her question after question, his sharp blue eyes boring into her like awls: Can you describe the van? Can you describe the men? What did they say to you? What did they do? Did they say anything to each other? Mention any names? Did you see the van's license plate? State? Color of the plate? Door on the side of the van or the back?

Her father, who had been there too, heard the tremor of exhaustion in her voice and finally said, "Back off, John," and Captain Hermann had looked surprised.

After a moment's pause, he had asked, "About these people who picked you up . . ."

Catherine shook her head. "I only saw—I only saw one of them," she said slowly. "And that was only the night he brought me back to New York."

Her first impulse had been to say nothing, to preserve a perfect and complete silence, but as a lawyer herself, she had seen that this would not do. It would raise more suspicions, if anything, and Captain Hermann, clearly a tenacious bulldog of a man, would never let her alone until she'd told him something. She'd had most of a day, once her mind was cleared of anesthetics, to come up with a story, though she would vastly have preferred to simply sleep, to forget.

But she would never forget. And she owed Vincent and his family more than she could ever repay, except by such means as this.

She only hoped her story wouldn't give Hermann any false clues or leads that might cause trouble for some innocent family of homeless people who undoubtedly had enough problems already.

Carefully, she went on, "They were—they were transients, they said. They couldn't get me to a hospital because I was bleeding too badly when they found me." That had been the one cut that wasn't on her face, a big vein in the forearm near the elbow, where she'd tried to protect herself.

"Well, why didn't they take you to a hospital later?" demanded Tom, from his post on the other side of the bed. It was his lunch hour—he looked like an ad in G.Q. "People like that are filthy, any of those cuts could have gotten infected."

Catherine sighed. "I don't know, but they were

probably afraid someone would accuse *them* of doing it."

That shut him up, at least for the time being.

Hermann left unsatisfied. Catherine deliberately made her description of her rescuers as vague as possible, insisted she had heard no names, and did her best to imply that the whole rescue had taken place several hours' drive outside New York City, reasoning that the van could just as easily have dumped her in the wilds of New Jersey as in the wilds of Central Park. She tried to cover everything, but the pain pills they were giving her made it hard to think—she could only do the best she could. Hermann had come back several times to the discrepancies in her story: her inability to describe clearly the room she had been in, or to identify any environmental noises; and most of all the neatness with which the facial wounds had been sutured, the obvious competence of the way her broken ribs had been strapped.

The door hadn't even quite closed behind the police officer when Tom started blustering. "It was sheer incompetence on his part that you weren't found before and spared all that! And I'm positive it was Hermann who leaked the story to the newspapers."

"Tom . . ." whispered Catherine pleadingly, sinking back on the pillows, exhausted by the questioning. They'd taken the bandages off her eyes that morning but the sensitive flesh was still swollen and discolored, and contact with the air smarted. The rest of her face was still covered.

"Really, Cathy, I can't afford that kind of publicity and neither can your father! God knows what else he'll tell reporters."

"Tom, please."

He'd stopped, then leaned down and, picking up her hand, kissed it. His hand was strong and smooth—like hers, unroughened by work of any kind. "I'm sorry," he said gently. "My white knight instincts coming to the fore. If there's anything I can do . . ."

But he didn't look at her eyes.

He left soon for a meeting with the construction company contracted for the new building, reassuring her as he left that she had only to name what she wanted, and he'd get it for her. The meeting was critical; they would be digging foundations soon. Her father had remained until she fell asleep.

Her face healed. Regarding herself in the powder room mirror of Il Forno, an upscale nouvelle Italian place on 43rd, she saw herself as she had always been: the smooth fair skin, the full lips and wide green eyes, the air of fragile delicacy. Only the look in the eyes had changed.

Her dust-blonde hair had been combed so that it lay forward over her ears to frame her face. Pushing it back, she considered for a moment the one scar they hadn't been able to remove, the one in front of her left ear. The cut had gone too deep, and lay too close to the veins and nerves to repair without a second operation, which she hadn't been willing to undergo. It was still an ugly red, though they told her it would pale later, enough to be concealed with makeup. Tom, on their dates, had subtly altered his body English so that he never kissed her on that side anymore.

She frowned, putting aside the vexed subject of Tom, and, collecting her purse, returned to the restaurant. Her father looked up from the two cappuccinos smoking gently on the table, and smiled his greeting.

"I've always wondered what goes on in those powder rooms," he said, and Catherine grinned back at him.

"All the witty repartee? The cutting remarks?"

"Exactly."

"Sort of like the men's room at your club?"

He drew himself up with mock dignity. "Now, that's a completely different matter."

"I've heard *that* before."

And he laughed, glad only to be with her. Even now, she thought, he had not fully recovered from her disappearance. These days he looked older, his face more lined beneath its shock of silver hair. Try as he would to pretend that the incident, being officially closed, had never taken place, like her he had learned that it could happen. She was truly all he had. The money, the apartment, the trips to Europe, the position in the firm and his careful quest to find among his younger business acquaintances a man who was exactly what she wanted—they were all part of the price he thought he had to pay to keep her in his life.

It made what she had to say all the harder.

She sipped her cappuccino, listening to the expertly timed ruffles and flourishes of the piano player across the room, almost buried under the muted hum of conversation. From her parents' instinctive graciousness and her own desire to please she had worked all her life to be kind and tactful in what she said, with the result that she hadn't the faintest idea how to lead up to a conversation she knew was going to hurt this man she loved.

Well, better go in with a belly flop than stand around wringing your hands on the shore.

"Dad," she said, setting down her cup and meeting his eyes, "I'm not going back to the firm."

His hand covered hers, warm and strong. "Of course you can have more time, darling. You can have all the time you need."

She had known he'd say that. She took a deep breath. "I mean not ever."

Before the frown pulled his silvery eyebrows down, before the defensive hardness appeared like a shield in his eyes, she saw it: he was hurt.

Quickly, she went on, "Dad, I was never very good at corporate law."

"Nonsense!" he blustered. "With your grades, and your mind? Why, nobody can be perfect just starting in!"

"I've been in it for two years and it's been a disaster. You know that."

He shook his head stubbornly, and she could see that he didn't know it—wouldn't know it—and was upset with her for bringing the matter up at all. "All you need is experience, Cathy."

"No." Her hands closed over his, holding them, willing him to listen and to believe her. "Things have changed."

"How?" he demanded, sounding like Tom. "What's changed?"

"Me," said Catherine. "What happened changed me." His eyes flicked aside. That too was something he didn't want to know. Subconsciously, she knew he didn't really want to be reminded that anything *had* happened. She leaned forward, forcing him to meet her eye. "You've got to accept that."

He said nothing, only looked at her with hurt

anger that he struggled not to show, lest something he say drive her further from him.

She went on slowly, trying to frame the thoughts that had been stirring in her for the past two months since she had come out of the hospital, trying to put them into words that he would understand—that she herself would comprehend. "When something like that happens, you see things differently. You see people suffering, see lives being destroyed . . . and it's all so *casual*. 'It happens . . .'" She shook her head, having put her finger on the thing that had appalled her most about the attack—that quality that had bordered upon absentmindedness, like swatting a roach.

"I want to help," she said, after a long hesitation. "Oh, I thought about things like the Peace Corps, or the Aid for the Homeless, but I've got skills. And I need—I don't know. Involvement with something real. There's injustice everywhere. I'm not the only person something like this has happened to."

"You're having a reaction to what happened," said Charles Chandler, quick as ever with a tactful explanation, a fresh coat of paint. "I understand that. Truly, I do." He took her hand again and patted it, as he had done when she was a teenager, or when she'd come home from college, frazzled and upset and lost in her search for something in her life that meant anything besides looking good and having a good time with her friends. "But that doesn't mean you have to throw away what you have. Don't be hasty, Catherine. You just need more time."

"I know what I need," she replied, and he looked away. "Dad, I can't go back to the way it was. I just—I've spent enough time hiding. And to run away from it now would be to hide forever."

On the other side of the room the piano player smoothed his way into "Smoke Gets In Your Eyes"; waiters in white coats steered among the dark sea of heads and cigarette-smoke like sails tacking through choppy waters before a storm. The earnest yammer of random conversation swirled around them: "Brewer's yeast and garlic, only it makes the cats smell like Italians . . ." "Do you have *any idea* how difficult it is to deal with the people in charge of that show?" ". . . which I can get for $44.95, y'see, 'cause I buy it wholesale." "Not a relationship, you nitwit, just a good, rousing, teeth-rattling . . ."

Her father started to draw his hand away, and she tightened her grip, holding it there. "And I need your encouragement," she said quietly.

He sat still for a long time, adjusting himself to that—thankful, perhaps, that she was asking him for something at least, something he could give her. Adjusting to the fact that she, not he, was responsible for her happiness.

At length his fingers returned the pressure of her hand. "I'd hoped . . ." He shrugged. "Well, maybe it was foolish. But I'd hoped you'd stay with the firm—that you'd be able to take it over one day. Every man wants his child to carry on for him. And I thought . . . That wasn't a fantasy, was it?"

She sighed, loving him, wishing it were possible to tell him in so many words that just because she wanted her own life didn't mean she was walking out of his. But she only said, "Not then it wasn't. But it's different now."

With Tom, it was less easy.

"Don't be ridiculous," he said, when she spoke of it to him as they walked back from dinner one night along 72nd Street toward Catherine's apartment on Central Park West. It was early July, and nine at night; the city wore twilight magic like a garment of flaming stars. In spite of conscientious workouts at the gym Tom always moved awkwardly, and when he was irritated this stiffness became more pronounced. Even his gestures had a jerky quality now, and in the shadows his brown eyes snapped with scorn.

"What, are you going to give up your apartment and live in a walk-up studio now because it's more politically correct? I know what you're doing, but I thought you'd have outgrown that kind of thing by your age. You feel you owe those hoboes or gypsies or whoever it was who picked you up—"

"And what if I do?" asked Catherine quietly, holding her spangled shawl close around her shoulders, the night breeze stroking back her hair.

"Oh, come on," he sniffed. "Be real."

She thought about those people she had never given a thought to before, the ones she had looked away from almost subconsciously: the old black woman who lingered by the post office steps, politely asking passersby for a quarter; the men sleeping stretched out with their heads on newspapers on the subway platforms; the children hanging around the doorways in Times Square because loitering in the night was better than going home. About the people who were only names in a newspaper: BROOKLYN MAN BEATEN AND ROBBED; TEENAGER RAPED; MOTHER OF THREE RAPED AND MURDERED; 81-YEAR-OLD NEWSVENDOR MUGGED . . .

"How much more real do you want to get?"

"I've tried poverty, Cathy," he said thinly. "I grew up counting pennies. You won't like it."

She turned her head, considering that smooth-shaven, angular face, those close lips, the beautiful lines of his gray wool suit and the pale pink silk of the shirt underneath. Well fed and well groomed and perfect, as she had always striven for perfection. Yes, he'd grown up with poverty, working in his father's restaurant and clerking at the local liquor store to pay for his college textbooks, and he never wanted to look upon it—or its results—again. "Poverty isn't what I'm looking for," she said quietly. "A way to help people is what I'm looking for. People who've been hurt, and who can't help themselves. And a way to stop this kind of thing from happening."

He rolled his eyes. "And what I'm saying is that the people who deserve help are usually the ones who get out and hustle, not the losers who go whining some kind of hard-luck story. Nobody *has* to starve in this world, Cathy. People can help themselves if they try."

"Now who's not being real?"

He made a soft sound, like a laugh, and put his arms around her, halting her on the sidewalk so that he could tilt his head a little and look down at her. He still favored, she couldn't help noticing, the right side, away from the scar.

"I just don't want to see you beat your head against a wall," he said gently. "And you will, if you follow up this harebrained idea of going into some kind of free legal aid clinic, or the D.A.'s office, or dishing out your services for free to whatever cause takes your fancy this week. I hate to tell you this, but you can't change the world, Cathy."

He bent his head, to lightly kiss her cheek. Though Catherine had dated several other men on an occasional basis—old friends, dinner-and-theater dates, dancing with Ed—Tom had been her only serious affair, certainly the only one she would consider marrying, as her father, she knew, wished she would do. Her father liked Tom.

But since her return, though Tom had started asking her out again as soon as her face had completely healed, they had not slept together. Neither had spoken of this, though Catherine could feel him waiting resentfully, and knew that he thought that this was the result of something which had taken place during those lost, mysterious ten days.

In point of fact, it was the quarrel at the Barron which had crystallized her reservations about the relationship—his possessiveness, his demands on her time, his desire to set her priorities for her. Occasionally she wondered whether his real objection to her finding a career other than that of being Charles Chandler's Daughter full-time stemmed from a feeling that the debutante daughter of a wealthy lawyer was a more prestigious catch than a working girl.

During the long days in the dark of the Tunnels, she had thought a good deal about Tom, though she had known even then that it was no time to come to any real conclusions. During the twenty-four hours between her return and her entry into the hospital for plastic surgery she had refused to see him, guessing instinctively what his reaction to her appearance would be and knowing herself unable to deal with it. Perhaps she had done him an injustice, she thought. But for whatever reasons, he had not tried to come until the operation was over. When he had asked her out again, she had resumed dating him, mostly from a desire to return to at least some of the life she had known before. And perhaps this relationship, now that she had lost most of her interest in dating other men, would be different, as other things were different for her.

But though he treated her as before, cherished her and gave her presents and accommodated her every request, she knew with absolute certainty that she had no further desire to take him into her bed. Even the fact that she had once done so—or felt ambivalent enough about him to let him talk her into doing so—seemed odd to her, like something which had taken place years ago, in somebody else's life.

Which was, in fact, the case.

Yet she could think of no good reason to break it off. He was certainly careful to give her no cause. And so she let things ride.

Still holding her—which she let him do, in spite of the fact that the grip, the strength, of any man's arms still made her tense up badly—he urged, "Don't punish yourself for what happened to you. Life goes on, you know."

A van swished by on 72nd, its headlights flashing across them as it passed the lamp on the corner. Catherine flinched slightly and looked, but it was old, yellow, and gay with free-form flowers like a '60s Tripsmobile. She stepped forward gently, disengaging herself from his arms. "I don't plan to."

She started toward her building, a tall, old-fashioned white structure whose wide blue-awninged windows faced the park. Tom stopped her, holding her by the arms. Quietly, his dark eyes intent now, he said, "You've never told me everything they did to you."

"How would you know whether what I told you was 'everything' or not?"

His grip tightened. "Did they rape you?"

Her gaze met his calmly. "Would it make that much difference to you?"

His eyes shifted. "Of course not." He took her hand again, and walked her to the door. "This isn't the time for you to be making life-decisions, Cathy," he said, as he bent to kiss her lips. "Don't do something we'll both regret."

"And the worst of it is, they might be right," she said the next day as she and Jenny walked along the shaded path toward the boathouse cafe in the park. The day was hot as only New York summer can be, muggy and still and unreal-feeling. Sunlight sparkled on the water, bobbing with paddleboats and little sails. Under yellow-and-orange parasols the wide terrace was crowded, the grass of the surrounding hillocks dotted with couples on blankets, with children and dogs playing Frisbee. On the other side of a scrim of trees what appeared to be the entire population of the free world sat in a gently steaming traffic-jam on Fifth Avenue.

"I mean, I might very well be subconsciously trying to—to make amends for being rich, for not wanting to see the ugliness and injustice around me. For being my father's daughter." She shoved her hands in the pockets of her light linen blazer, tipped her head to look up at her friend.

"I *know* I've spent my life not wanting to see ugly things, telling myself—like Dad does—that I can't do anything about violence and crime, so why upset myself by dwelling on them. But I feel different now. I want to help—I want to . . . to do something so that what happened to me won't happen to other people. But on the other hand, I *might* subconsciously feel that I somehow deserved what happened to me. *Damn* those Psych 101 courses at Radcliffe, anyhow!"

And Jenny had laughed. "I know. Every time I edit a self-help book I start wondering if I'm doing things from some hidden drive. But does it matter?" She shook back her straight dark hair. "If you can get pleasure, or even just satisfaction, from doing what you do—if you're helping people—does it matter why you do it? It's your life. You're not accountable to them, you know."

"I know," she sighed. "*They* haven't quite got that yet, but *I* have." She shrugged, and scuffed at a rock with the toe of her Reebok. Neither Jenny nor Nancy—who'd come down to spend the week with her after she'd gotten out of the hospital—had ever asked her about those missing ten days. She didn't know whether they'd heard her story secondhand from her father or not, though she suspected they had. If the positions were reversed she knew *she* would certainly be curious. But she was grateful for their silence on the subject.

"Enough of this soul searching," she said, shaking her head. "No job is cast in concrete. If I hate it I can always be a cocktail waitress."

"No, no!" objected Jenny gravely. "You have to wear those awful shoes with the four-inch heels."

"Right," agreed Catherine, who had never, not even in her college days, had to wait tables in her life. "One of those drive-ups where you wear roller skates, then. Let's go get a soda."

It was curious, she thought later, as she walked back home along the edge of the park, how deliciously good it was simply to be outside, to feel the sun and the air on her face. Vincent had spoken of that, too . . . of how he had never been outside in the daytime, nor seen the daisies in the park grass when they were open to the sun.

His was a world of dusk and night. A world of silence—it had taken her weeks to reaccustom herself to the continual din of voices and telephones, to the roar and stink of traffic and the thunder of passing planes.

A world whose inhabitants would pick up and help a human being they found lying on the ground as unhesitatingly as the average New Yorker would walk around one.

She had come gradually to fully understand the gift that Vincent and his family in the Tunnels had given her: the gift of trust. Maybe not trust in everything—maybe not the innocent trust she had once had, the assumption that everything was all right and would be all right . . . but trust in the goodness of humankind in spite of the world as it stood. Her innate trust in life, her ability to enjoy the world without fear, though wounded, had not been killed.

Because Vincent had been kind.

She thought a great deal about Vincent. She missed him desperately; missed having him to talk to, missed hearing his voice and knowing he was near. In the ten days they had known one another she had felt closer to him than she'd felt to anyone she had ever met, man or woman, as if they had been friends for years, forever. To him she could say anything, and know he would understand.

For weeks she subconsciously looked for him, half expecting to see him somewhere, though she knew that he had never, would never, could never emerge from his underground world. Once at one of Tom's expensive corporate parties she'd heard a woman across the room call out his name, and had spun to look. But of course it wasn't him, just a good-looking Italian punk, bodyguard to one of Tom's shadier contractors. And the name Vincent was common enough. But the incident brought to her a little pang of regret.

The world Below was closed to her, as that Above was forever off-limits to him. Nevertheless, she found herself looking twice when she'd pass the big cement drainage culverts in Central Park, half expecting . . . she didn't know what. And going about the city in the sunlight, to her father's brownstone for tea in the warm, gluey twilights or to the corner cafe for coffee with her friends, when she passed by the grille of a sidewalk steam-vent, she would smile.

Eight

Well, her credentials are excellent." New York District Attorney John Moreno flipped through the neatly printed résumé which lay on the desk before him, on top of a barely controlled chaos of depositions, arrest reports, case files, briefs, affidavits, transcripts, copies of transcripts, copies of the copies, and conflicting memos on various subjects from the mayor and the chief of police. Moreno was a big, sallow man with the slightly harried expression of those who deal with justice in large cities; he was in shirt sleeves, the air conditioner being on the fritz for the fifth time since Easter. As a major official in city hierarchy he rated a sizable office in the crowded justice department—and a secretary, though the poor woman seemed to spend most of her time fielding phone calls and scheduling appointments—and if its plain glass rectangle of window looked, not out onto the beautiful cement cloverleaf of the access ramps of the Brooklyn Bridge but into the swarming beehive of glass-partitioned cubicles and scuffed beige file cabinets that made up the division's central bull pen, who was he to rail at the ways of an imperfect world?

"Radcliffe, Cornell Law, two years' experience in corporate." He glanced through the interior window's open mini-blinds at the woman who sat in the miniscule waiting-area outside his office, slender, blonde, and stunningly beautiful in a simple black suit he could tell at a glance hadn't come out of Macy's basement. "She really wants a job?"

Joe Maxwell, perched with one flank on the other side of his desk, followed his glance. "She says so. Who knows?" He shrugged.

One of the younger deputies of the division, Joe had come in with a ready-made veneer of cynicism that had quickly toughened to case-hardened steel. He too was in shirt sleeves—at least Moreno's office had a circular fan all its own for when the air conditioners quit, which the offices of the deputies didn't.

Maxwell went on, "She's some rich guy's daughter . . . looking for something 'meaningful,' I guess. You remember, the one who disappeared this spring. Tom Gunther's girlfriend."

"Oh, yeah?" During the ten days of her absence Gunther had made an absolute nuisance of himself, both here and at the police station, blustering, threatening, and heckling as to why something wasn't being done. And then he'd come back in a lather demanding to know who in the office had leaked the story to the papers, as if his own performance hadn't been sufficient tip-off to the ambulance-chasers in the lobby.

Moreno took another look. The details of the

case, if he'd ever known them, had long been wiped out of his mind by two months of murder, rape, wholesale drug-dealing and organized theft, but the woman looked like she'd be worth that kind of a floor show. And if the résumé was anything to go by, she was far from the society bimbo he'd subconsciously pictured at the time.

He shrugged. "It's a pair of hands," he said. "It's a brain. God knows we could use the help."

Outside, deputy D.A.s and clerks were scurrying around like ants in a hosed-out anthill, one step ahead of the impossible task of providing, as the pledge says, justice for all. Ms. Chandler glanced back over her shoulder at the confusion now and then, but she seemed calm. Moreno wondered whether that was genuine levelheadedness or just the illusion that all this wasn't going to have anything to do with her. She didn't look like a flake, but then neither had that Vassar chick in research who'd turned out to be a semi-finalist in the Tri-State Nail Polishing Championships.

Joe made a gesture that clearly said, *It's your funeral, pal*. "So where do you want to put her?"

"Out in the field," said Moreno simply, reaching for a cigarette and then remembering that today was the first day of a new life, and picking up and chewing a toothpick instead. *Keep reminding yourself of that, Johnny*, he told himself. "Research, investigation, whatever. Give her all the legwork. Throw everything at her. If she's any good we'll find out."

"Right." Joe's boyish face wore a look of wry amusement as he hopped off the corner of the desk and went to open the door. "Ms. Chandler . . . District Attorney Moreno will see you now."

* * *

The first two weeks were awful.

Though sheltered as a child, Catherine had never been deliberately blind. In college, when she was dating the indignantly radical Simon, she had gone through a brief period of intensive study of all the world's injustices, though she admitted to herself later this had been mostly to stay in the running with him and his friends. But even during that phase poverty and crime had been a matter of academic knowledge, for it is difficult to acquire a deep anger at the capitalist system while living on what one's father sends every month. And once she'd broken off with Simon, her dutiful newspaper-reading tended more and more to alternate between the business section, the fashion pages, and entertainment.

This, as she had known it would be, was different.

It was personal now. She knew, "of her own knowledge," as her professors of criminal law had always said, what it was to be a victim, what it was to be helpless in the power of others—and what the city could do. Knowing it, she could never pretend she didn't know. Having survived it, she knew she could not turn her back on others who had suffered.

But only when she stepped out of the insulated and luxurious world of high-finance corporate law did she come to realize what her decision meant in terms of the ugliness, the violence, the harshness of the city of which she had barely been aware.

In Investigations, she learned about things like unheated tenement rooms where the rust-clogged sinks yielded more roaches than water, where toilets hadn't flushed for decades and children routinely checked out their rooms with hammers for rats before bedding down for the night; about eight-year-olds with hundred-dollar-a-day coke habits peddling crack on the schoolgrounds; about the men who casually supplied them.

In Research she learned how easy it was to evade the law, which was bound by paperwork and the technicalities of ensuring that the innocent did not suffer while the guilty hired lawyers to plea-bargain them through the cracks; she learned that it was generally the small-time crooks who went to jail while the big-timers, the drug dealers, the organizational bosses and the gang chiefs, had the power to go free.

She learned for the first time what the inside of jails looked like, the pale cement and the eternal metal grillwork of the Tombs, the open toilets, the lack of privacy or dignity or quiet, the scrawled graffiti and the terrifying smell of sweat, excrement, and free-floating hate. She learned how innocent the bland-faced guilty could seem, and how easy it is to misread fear as guilt.

She learned, too, what a terrifying amount of paperwork was required of those who upheld the law: reports to be filed where they could be found again when the offender's case finally went on trial, sometimes months or years after the incident; transcripts that got thrown out of court because someone hadn't bothered to read a man his rights; police reports, probation reports, juvenile authority reports that all had to be checked, filed, rewritten, kept up to date, brought to somebody's attention, laid on somebody's desk.

She learned, in fact, about the whole terrifying, top-heavy and inefficient machinery designed to intermesh justice with law, and about the people who came in contact with that machinery, on both sides of the law. As they said, she learned the ropes.

After the first week of trying to find a parking place—having discovered that her permit was no guarantee there'd be space in the garage—she started taking the bus to work, coming in early because of the sheer volume of work that had to be on the D.A.'s desk by noon. Usually she stayed late, and rode home feeling as if she'd been in a fight. It seemed that no matter which division she was working in that day someone was always demanding where some report or transcript was (*We gotta get that in by tomorrow, you know*). The number of telephone calls that interrupted her work made it worse—some days, it seemed, half the morning went by with nothing but a sore ear to show for it, and then there'd be Joe Maxwell standing in front of her desk saying, "Dammit, Radcliffe, you've had those figures for days."

She learned the trick of getting showered, dressed, and made-up in thirty minutes in the morning—she who had previously required an hour and a half before she figured it was adequate—and longed for the leisure to read the paper over breakfast—or even *get* breakfast in the quiet of her apartment. Most days it was a bagel or a take-out Egg Zowie from the Roach Coach that set up shop on the near edge of City Hall Park at ten. Yet it seemed that she was perpetually late, perpetually behind schedule, perpetually hanging someone else up because try as she would she was never good enough.

Her father had been right, she thought. Tom had been right. Sitting wearily one evening in her cubicle—actually no more than a corner of the bull pen, hemmed in by filing cabinets and one glass-paneled partition-wall—she listened wearily to the cleaning staff systematically upending trashcans into their bins in the lowered lights of after-hours. She had shattered her life, thrown away all the comfort, all the peace she had known, and for what? To chase a dream she wasn't even good at.

The place was insufferably hot—the air conditioning was still out—and stank of old cigarettes; she felt sweaty and messy and her head and legs ached. The woman whose abusive husband they'd been trying to serve papers on for two weeks had decided to go back to him after all. The dealer picked up outside the gates of Abraham Lincoln Grade School had just walked on a technicality—he'd be back passing out crack again in the morning. The young man who'd seen a pimp cut up a sixteen-year-old girl with a razor had decided on the witness stand that contrary to what he'd said in his statement to the police, he hadn't really seen anything—he'd been out in the alley taking a leak.

She had six more reports to write and she was tired to the marrow of her bones.

At least I'm improving, she though wanly. *It took me two years in Dad's offices to figure out I was a failure. Now I've got my time down to two weeks.*

She leaned her head on her hand and sighed. A tear splatted on the triplicate yellow/pink/green form in front of her, and she brushed it away impatiently. *Dammit*, she thought. *I DO want to do this, but I've never learned how*. It wasn't the law itself—she knew the law. It was the people, and the pressure, and the frustration of seeing all her work unraveled even as she labored frantically to get it done.

Maybe all she *was* qualified for was to be Daddy's Little Girl—sorry, that should be Charles Chandler's Daughter. To finagle her way neatly through the ins and outs of torts and rights-of-way; to dress well, be beautiful, attend parties and impress clients. To keep track of clean little legalities that didn't change their minds, or disappear, or get arrested for Drunk and Disorderly, or turn out to not have Green Cards or to have been lying all along. She'd be no more happy than she had been before, but at least she'd be able to sleep in now and then.

A shadow loomed in the door of the bull pen. "You still here, Radcliffe?"

She swiped a finger under her eye quickly and stammered, "I'm just finishing up."

"At seven-thirty I should hope to shout you would be." Joe Maxwell took a step closer and peered at her in the yellow glare of the desk lamp. With his coat off, his tie stuffed in one pocket, and his dark hair rumpled, he looked considerably less formidable than he did during work hours. "You had dinner?"

She shook her head—nor lunch, she realized, now that she thought about it. No wonder she had a headache.

"Come on," he said. "Let's go get a hamburger. You look like your blood sugar needs a boost."

"It isn't that," she said, sinking ten minutes later into the turquoise vinyl of a booth at Tummy Time, a storefront greasy spoon on Reade. "It's just that I can't seem to do any of it *right*. I just barely have time to scribble in reports—they're never right—I'm always late meeting witnesses—everybody has to check back with me because of something I left out, or forgot . . . I lose things. I never used to be like this."

She had dreamed about Vincent last night: dreamed about standing in the dark of the sub-basement with him, the strong pressure of his arm enfolding her waist, the scratchy softness of his coat beneath her cheek. There had been two doors leading out of that cellar, not one, and she had had to choose which to take, not knowing where either of them led. She had kept asking him, *Which should I take?* and he had shaken his head and said, *You know where you must go.*

Tears started in her eyes again. Joe pulled a paper napkin from the tin dispenser on the tabletop and handed it to her. She turned away from him, ashamed of her weakness.

"Radcliffe," said Joe after a moment, "let me give you a hypothetical situation." His voice was crisp and cynical as usual, but not impatient. Above the counter someone had the Mets–Cubs game on the wide-screen TV, the noise like a texture in the hot and gritty air. At the next table three guys in gray coveralls like mechanics discussed the metaphysical properties of matter over a couple of beers; a pair of button-down Wall Street types in a booth discreetly contemplated the waitress's breasts as she brought Maxwell and Catherine their food.

"Now picture in your mind," Joe went on, an instinctive courtroom timing in his light tenor voice, "the entire accumulated by-products of the Chicago stockyards piled up in a one-mile cube on a piece of ground that you, and I, and the other deputy D.A.s in the division, are required to clear away with shovels by the first of next week. And every morning at seven o'clock, a fleet of a hundred dump trucks arrives with fresh contributions to add to the problem.''

He leaned forward, dark eyes grave, and gestured with his teaspoon. ''Do you honestly think that under the circumstances anyone is seriously going to criticize the quality of your shoveling?''

Catherine turned away, hiding her spurt of laughter behind her hand.

''Lighten up, Radcliffe.'' Joe smiled. ''You're doing fine.''

It had been a long road back. There were still things that bothered her, caught her unawares, made her realize she'd been much more of a princess than she'd thought at the time: her constant distaste at the black sludge of office coffee after her own neat routine of grinding gourmet beans to make it fresh to her taste at home; her miffed indignation when she realized that, having only been hired in July, she wasn't going to get a vacation in August like everyone else, and would be stuck in the unventilated sweatbox of the office doing double coverage while everyone else went to the beach.

Her father came down from their country place on Gloucester Island that sweltering weekend, and took her, Tom, and Kim Baskerville, the widow of an old friend, out to dinner and to a Chopin recital at Lincoln Center. This was a major sacrifice on his part, Catherine realized, considering how much he hated New York in the summer.

''Your father doesn't admit it,'' Kim said to her, falling into step with Catherine as they came down the steps into the clammy night, ''but he is proud of you, you know.''

Catherine stared at her in surprise. Kim was a pretty little wren of a woman, with a healthily tanned face set off by the subdued silver-shot black of her dress, and snow-white hair. After a moment she said, "I thought . . . I was afraid he'd be angry."

"Oh, he was." Kim smiled. Ahead of them, Tom was tipping the parking valet for his car. A line of headlights blazed behind, and ahead at the end of the drive Amsterdam Avenue was a river of twinkling gold. "And he misses meeting you for dinner and drinks when he gets through at the office. He feels . . . a little hurt. He's told me so."

Now that she thought of it, Catherine realized, looking across at the older woman's serene little face, her father had mentioned Kim quite frequently in conversation lately. An old family friend—Catherine had been well into her twenties before she'd been able to break herself of calling her "Mrs. Baskerville" and had only done so when Kim had threatened to slap her hand if she did it again—she was a woman of his own world, much more so than Catherine was these days. She knew the latest on which family friends were doing what, who had daughters making their debuts or getting married, all the country-club gossip he missed being able to confide. Perhaps, she thought suddenly, he had needed to be freed from being her father as much as she had needed to be free of being his child.

Kim's eyes met hers, twinkling. For a moment the two women looked at each other in perfect understanding and complicity. Then Catherine took her hand and squeezed it with a smile, and they walked together down the steps toward the car.

"But you know," Kim went on quietly, "this

summer up at Gloucester"—she had kept her
husband's place up there, Catherine knew, they
had been summer neighbors as well as city
friends—"he's talked about 'My daughter in the
D.A.'s office.' Or he'll say, 'Oh, she works too
hard—harder than she ever did for me.' But as he
says it he'll sort of puff himself up—you know how
he does—and there's this shine in his eyes. Any
man can protect and care for his child, you know,
but not every man can raise her to be strong."

Her father helped Kim into the backseat of Tom's
Mercury Town Car, and Catherine into the front
next to Tom. Tom smiled at her. He had sent her
flowers at the office that day, the only bright spot
in an otherwise gruesome struggle against a heat-
aggravated avalanche of work. As the vehicle edged
slowly into the shining lava-flow of traffic Catherine
heard her father's soft voice from the rear seat,
comparing notes about the recital with Kim, and
talking about the trip back to the country
tomorrow. Catherine looked out the window and
smiled.

This was what it was, then, to come back to life.

And yet as they passed the dark trees of Central
Park she wondered suddenly where Vincent was,
and what he was doing, and whether he was
happy or sad. He would have enjoyed the recital,
she thought—he'd told her once that Chopin was
one of his favorites, and that there was no one in
the Tunnels who played Chopin properly. And it
seemed as if some hollow place in her heart echoed
with the whisper of his name.

In the basement of the Faber Mutual Trust on
Wall Street a Puerto Rican janitor shoved a wheeled
canvas bin into the elevator, and hit the button for

the 20th floor. The machinery cut in with an almost soundless, heavy-muscled whir. In the bottom of the sub-basement shaft the oiled wheels turned, the cables lifted smoothly, taking the car's weight unnoticed up the narrow darkness of the shaft. The machinery was designed to raise two tons beyond the weight of the car itself; the form that clung to the cables a few feet beneath the mechanisms of the car's subfloor was as nothing.

Vincent knew elevators well. The dizzy black well of the shaft beneath his feet didn't trouble him, for like the machinery of the lift, his hands and shoulders were strong enough to take many times his own weight. Little squares of light from each floor passed skimmed down his face and the dark patches of his coat, glinted on the hardware of his belt and in the tourmaline depths of his eyes. He had spent the evening patrolling the Tunnels, wandering farther and farther from the inhabited areas, exploring as his feet willed: watching, as most of the young men of the community watched on their patrols, for evidence of water leakage or the subterranean quicksands that patched Manhattan's geology, for anomalous tracks that might spell danger or trouble to the dwellers Below, or problems with the metal gates and doors. With everything makeshift, everything acquired third-hand when no one else wanted it and forever on the verge of dissolution, this kind of vigilance was an eternal task.

He had visited the dark, chaotic threshold of the Abyss, where endless stairs spiraled down into nothingness; the vast Chamber of the Winds, that pillared, silent temple seven hundred feet below the city's subfloors, where the old voodoo witch Narcissa dwelt with her demons and her spells; the beauty of the Painted Tunnels where old Elizabeth worked by candlelight, covering the bare walls in colors. An endless kingdom, of which he was guardian and child.

Later in the evening, when he was sure no one would be about to see, he would walk hooded in Central Park, his only chance to touch, even at second hand, the glittering, complex life of the city, to taste the sweetness of night air among water and trees. But it was still too early for that.

Nevertheless, the restlessness of the summer night was on him. And so he had come here.

The elevator stopped. Leaning out from the cables still gripped in one iron paw, Vincent reached into the recess in the wall of the shaft and threw the emergency manual lever used by the repairmen. The doors of the nineteenth floor opened, and he swung himself lightly over the abyss to the threshold and stepped out into a service corridor. The offices of the nineteenth floor were deserted by this time of night—a fact he had observed over the months, as he observed everything in the nighttime city—and his soft boots made no sound on the bare concrete floor, his vast black mantle barely a rustle against a window's frame.

The Faber Trust was an old building, constructed in the thirties and modernized several times since. It pyramided upwards like an impossibly elongated ziggurat, rather than rising in straight black glassy columns like more modern structures, and its walls were a clifflike warren of ledges, crannies, perches, gargoyles and ornaments. The pigeons nesting in the decorative triangle of level space behind one of its outthrusts of masonry knew Vincent well, and didn't even take their heads from beneath their wings.

Vincent settled his broad shoulders to the rising wall behind him, rested his elbows on his drawn-up knees. Before him the city lay, a prodigal jewelbox of lights.

Like Mohammed on the hill above Damascus, he could only look. He knew that this alien beauty was not for him. To his left, almost within touching-distance of his hand, it seemed, the double shaft of the World Trade Center towered far above his already lofty seat, obsidian towers wreathed in electric flame. Beyond the tangly colored chaos of the Village and Chinatown he could pick out the gold-stitched needle of the Empire State Building, the deco flamboyance of the Chrysler, Broadway like a thick rope of light.

Dante had spoken of a scene like this, he recalled; circling down through darkness to the fire-carpeted velvet of the floor of Hell upon a monster's back. Had it looked like this?

Or had it been less beautiful?

Her world.

The noise of the city came up around him, transmuted by distance into a throbbing clamor like the sea—or like the sea as it was described in Father's books. To Vincent's hyperacute sense of smell the night was burningly alive, acrid with car exhaust, fetid with the shimmering rivers of fire-spangled obsidian on either side of the blazing island, and wild with the dizzy enchantment of free air.

She was down there somewhere. Happy, he thought, reaching tentatively out toward her. He felt her contentment, her well-being, like the echo of distant music.

The greatest love, Plato had said, is that which wills happiness to the beloved for the beloved's own sake. It was all he could do for her, now.

When she had stepped through that door, walked into that column of downstreaming light, she had gone out of his world and out of any possibility of coming in contact with his world again. She had spoken of her own father, a man of great kindness and love, and of friends she cared for. The newspaper article Father had shown him had mentioned a boyfriend as well. She had gone back to them, back to that world of flaming frenetic beauty—back to the lands of light—to be made whole.

He should, he knew, be glad.

Gazing out over the twinkling splendor of the city of lights, he had never felt lonelier in his life.

Nine

Isaac Stubbs's Academy of Streetfighting was situated in one of the shadier East Side districts not too far from the city, state, and federal purlieus to the south, a neighborhood some of its inhabitants compared unfavorably with a demilitarized zone. Catherine paid off her cab and glanced again at the piece of paper with the address, then looked around her at the grimy brown-brick loft-buildings, the gutters filled with old newspapers and broken glass, the chipped and filthy sidewalks. Even at this hour of the morning the place looked far from prepossessing—what it would be like at night she didn't care to contemplate. Across the street in what looked like a converted fire station someone was overhauling a disreputable Cadillac ambulance; to her right a bleary sign advertised rooms for single men only; a window down the block bore the faded inscription *S. Pliskin: New York Tours.* In the open vestibule of the building an old man in rags slept peacefully.

Doubtfully, Catherine climbed the steps to the third floor loft and went in.

"Mr. Stubbs?" she called out.

The loft was dim, its windows facing west and north, away from the morning sun. A part of it had been fitted up as living quarters, Spartan and yet curiously sophisticated: a worn gray couch that had been expensive when it was new, a low table made of plate glass and orange crates, a steel lamp. The dwellers in the Tunnels obviously weren't the only ones in New York to make a living by what the richer world tossed away. Two things were not secondhand: the crossed katanas that graced one wall, and a minimalist abstract bronze of a woman's torso that her expert eye placed at well over two thousand dollars, a statement not only about the owner's taste, but his priorities. Somewhere music was playing, single-trumpet jazz, spare and gentle and cool.

"Is anybody here?" She stepped beyond into the rest of the loft, dim and cavernous under unlit steel industrial lamps and bare iron beams. Mats covered the floor, some of canvas, others the hard woven straw of the traditional Japanese tatamis. In a corner a weight bench held a neatly graded set of hand-barbells. Elsewhere a life-sized wall-target displayed the lethal attack-points of the human body. Leather punching- and kicking-bags and assorted practice-dummies dangled on chains from the ceiling, stirring a little in the breeze from the door and giving the place an eerie sense of habitation.

"Well, we know *you're* here," said a soft voice behind her.

Catherine whirled, for a split second back in the alley, facing again the men in the van.

A stocky black man reached out of the shadow of one of the practice-dummies and pulled a string, turning on an overhead light.

If she'd encountered him on the street a year ago Catherine would have given him wide berth, quickened her step and kept a firm hand on her purse. He looked like trouble, until you saw his smile.

"You should always know what's comin' up behind you," he admonished gently, and she felt the warm brown eyes travel quickly over her, checking out details in the way she'd seen cops do: pricing her suit, shoes, earrings, and purse, not as a thief would, but to get whatever information he could. Then his smile widened. "This time it's *good* news."

He held out his hand, callused and rough, like a slab of pickled leather, but clean. "I'm Isaac—Isaac Stubbs."

She smiled back. "Catherine Chandler."

He had a lot of little crescent-shaped scars near his eyes and on his broad cheekbones, and there was a gap in one side of his smile. His close-cropped woolly hair was gray at the temples. He was a man who'd been around the dark side of the moon. He tipped his head a little to one side, considering her. "So you want to learn to take care of yourself."

"That's right."

The coffee-dark gaze went over her, reading and understanding what he saw. Though she had her hair brushed forward she knew he noted the scar, but only in passing; to him it was less important than what he saw in her eyes. "Because something bad happened to you."

It was not a question, not a guess, but she nodded, confirming what he already knew.

"And you don't want anything like that to ever happen again."

116

She said quietly, "Never."

They had her in Investigations again that week, out in the field: interviewing, hunting down witnesses, collecting facts—by herself this time. In the cheap bars, the dirty grocery stores, the dark tenement hallways that stank of urine and rats, her fear had come back. But this time it wasn't the paralyzing nightmare fear that still whispered to her sometimes when, as she walked along a sidewalk, a van would pass by on the street. This was, she realized, the perfectly rational awareness that if any of those unshaven men with glittery eyes who passed her in the shadowed halls of the railroad flats, if any of those arrogant gangs of teenagers she had to speak to on streetcorners, were to seize her, she wouldn't have the faintest idea what to do.

The experience outside the Barron Hotel had taught her one thing unforgettably: the appalling and unexpected strength of a man's hands.

She was small, she was pretty, and if she stayed with the D.A.'s office she was likely to be doing a lot of that kind of investigation in the future. It was time, she thought, rationalizing a desire that had been forming in her mind since she'd left the Tunnels, that she picked up another job skill.

"Okay," said Isaac, reading all that and more in her eyes. He stepped around the hanging dummy, his movements graceful as some incredibly powerful dancer's. "Now, I don't teach none of that Oriental stuff," he warned her. "No Kung Fu, no Egg Foo Yung. I'm from New York City, and what I teach is New York City street-fighting, mean and dirty. The only philosophy that counts around here is doin' whatever it takes to come out alive. You use what you got . . . lemme see your shoe."

Startled, Catherine caught the nearest kicking bag for balance and removed one high-heeled shoe. She was dressed for work, having taken off early on her lunch hour to seek out the place. Already no command of this man's, however bizarre, seemed out of place or open to question.

"You can kill a man with your shoe," remarked Isaac, and without so much as looking behind him, whipped his arm back, driving the three-inch spike of the heel into the temple of the man-shaped canvas dummy a few paces to his rear. The heel pierced the tough cloth easily. The plastic pellets that filled the bag leaked slowly out, rattling on the mat below.

"It's not fancy," said Isaac mildly, handing the weapon back to her, "and it ain't pretty, but it works . . . if you got the stomach for it."

Dad would have a stroke, thought Catherine, watching in a kind of gruesome fascination the slow leak of pellets from the lolling head of the facsimile man. *No—Dad would not even be able to conceive what this is all about. And Tom . . .*

She took a deep breath. "When do we start?"

And Isaac, seeing he had judged her right, smiled.

Dammit, I WILL not be late again, thought Catherine grimly, hurrying her steps through the fluorescent bustle of the NYPD Computer Data Center. *I don't care if that woman DID take forever giving her deposition. And I've still got—what?—how many leads to run down on the Perez case?* She glanced at her watch, confirming that she had enough time to collect what she needed here and make it back to Moreno's office by two. *That woman on the BIF System will KILL me when I come in with another rush request.*

The Data Center occupied an entire floor of police headquarters, and seemed a world apart from the slightly grimy, dingy quarters of the other divisions above and below. Perhaps, thought Catherine, it's because the equipment is more modern than the rest of the place, or because of the faintly science-fictional air—or maybe only because computers had to be kept clean to operate. The place was no less crowded, no less busy, than the rest of the department, but it was quieter here. Now and then, over the muted hum of the operators' voices, rose the chatter of a printer. The frenzied need for documentation and paper-pushing was no less urgent here; most of the paper was just invisible.

She found the station she needed. The woman there glanced up. A few years younger than Catherine, she was less well but far more trendily dressed, her mahogany-colored African hair braided tightly in a thick mass of cornrows. Her bronze lips tightened in irritation as she recognized Catherine.

"Edie," said Catherine, "do you have those addresses for me yet?"

"Yeah." Edie pulled a long printout from the top of her OUT basket. "I got 'em." She thrust them at her. "Here, take 'em."

"Thanks." Catherine folded them across, slipped them into her briefcase which held, in addition to her papers these days, the folded-up sweats she wore on the infrequent occasions she could make it down to Isaac's. She hadn't been all week, and what with the Perez case it didn't look like she'd make it there anytime soon, unless she started getting up at five. "I appreciate it."

"Yeah, you *should* appreciate it," retorted Edie. "Considerin' I been doin' all your work."

Catherine stopped, broken out of her own concerns by the obvious resentment in Edie's voice. *Damn*, she thought, *stepped on someone's toes AGAIN*. "I'm sorry," she said, looking down at the dark girl sitting behind the cool plastic block of the monitors. "The D.A.'s really got me running. They're testing me."

"Who you kidding?" Scorn flickered in Edie's cinnamon eyes as she looked her up and down. "I know the way you uptown girls operate. You swing in here, shed a few tears for humanity . . . and then you go shopping."

She, like Joe Maxwell, had obviously seen a lot of bleeding hearts in her time. Catherine reflected that back in her college-radical days—all three months of them—the accusation would probably have been true. But the thought of the hamburgers wolfed down at her high-piled desk at seven at night and the terrifying proportions to which the pile of dirty laundry in her apartment had grown because she hadn't had a half hour to spare in the last week made her laugh in spite of herself. She couldn't remember the last time she'd had the leisure to go shopping for so much as a quart of milk.

"That's not true."

"It's not, hunh?" Edie's full lips twisted. "Catherine Chandler." She glanced at Catherine's security badge for spelling. "Let's check you out."

"Most people call me Cathy," said Catherine quietly, as Edie turned back to her terminal and punched in keys.

The BIF spread sheet was a first-line search system, accessing information on names that could be later followed up in the files—or more often by sheer legwork—for more detailed data. Knowing the speed at which the in-putters worked, which varied from glacial all the way up to snaillike, Catherine doubted her employment statistics from the D.A.s office would be in the system yet. Probably just as well, she thought, since it was precisely the employment record a bleeding-heart rich girl would have.

But something did come out of the files, after all.

VICTIM NAME—CATHERINE CHANDLER

DATE OF INCIDENT—APRIL 12, 1986

VICTIM ACCOUNT—FACE SEVERELY SLASHED WITH KNIFE OR RAZOR, PUNCHED AND KICKED ABOUT THE BODY AND HEAD. UNCONSCIOUS BODY DUMPED IN CENTRAL PARK BY THREE CAUCASIAN MALES AT APPROX 11:30 P.M.

FILE NO—ADRX 71423

The screen flickered, dissolved into a brief cubist checkerboard of grays, whites, and blacks, then assembled itself into a digitalized fax of the one photograph the police had taken of her in her apartment that first night.

For the records.

Edie gasped. "Oh, my God."

She looked up at Catherine in genuine horror, pity, and shame for having pulled the thing into the light from the storage files' anonymous guts. "Oh, Cathy, I'm sorry . . ."

Having seen it live in her mirror for twenty-four ugly hours, Catherine could view the picture dispassionately, but she had to admit it was pretty bad. "Don't be," she said with a rueful smile. "It's an old picture."

But later she had the file pulled.

It was partly out of morbid curiosity, almost like reading a review of a play she had been in, or an old love letter to someone who no longer mattered. She hadn't known how to go about it before, but she'd made a mental note of the file number from the screen. As a member of the D.A.'s staff, she told herself, she had every right to see it. Taking the folder out of her desk that night after all but one of tomorrow's case reports had been completed—she would, she vowed with a mental sigh and a glance at the clock, come in early yet again tomorrow and finish that last one—she was reminded of the hero in *Jaws* proposing to undertake some slightly extralegal activity in the middle of the night: *I can do anything I want, I'm the chief of police.*

The picture in the file was as gruesome as it had been on Edie's computer screen that afternoon.

She put it aside and thumbed quickly through the reports, Tom's account of the party at the Barron, her father's description of her and her habits, transcripts of her own three interviews with Captain Hermann and his brief and almost unintelligible notes about them, searching for the information she had really pulled the file to find: whether or not anything had been gleaned about the Tunnels, and if anything was being done to follow up.

Victim was deliberately vague and unhelpful concerning the transients she claimed cared for her after the incident.

(*"She claimed!"* thought Catherine indignantly. *Where do they think I was, out on the tiles someplace?!?*)

Victim refused to identify location where she spent ten days following the assault, could not give descriptions; claimed her eyes were covered until she was driven back to New York and released close to own address on Central Park West.

It was obvious—in fact it had been obvious to her even when Hermann interviewed her in the hospital, with her father and Tom standing by—that he found her story suspiciously thin.

But it was equally clear that he had formed no conclusions about where she *had* been—that she had given nothing away that might lead him, or anyone else, to that quiet world of darkness and softly clanging pipes, the world where, as Vincent had said, those who had fled the city's cruelties lived as well as they could. She had done as she had promised, and guarded the secret of their lives.

She closed up the folder, preparing to slip it into the bottom of somebody else's file tray for the clerks to return it to obscurity in the morning. As she did so the final page of it caught her eye.

Insufficient evidence. Status: Inactive.

Inactive.

That meant, she thought, as she walked from the bus around the corner to her building, that what had happened to her, the incident that had ripped her life in two—that could so easily have finished her—had become simply "one of those things."

It meant they'd never caught the three men who'd made of her face what that picture had shown. That they were still free. And that nobody was looking for them anymore.

She thought about that picture, sitting at her dressing table forty-five minutes later, face washed, teeth brushed, unwinding before going to bed.

The cool Wedgwood colors of the room were lost in lamplight and shadow. The French doors onto the terrace stood open, in the hopes of catching a breeze, but the white gauze curtains hung straight. The September night was like tepid glue. From down below, the murmur of traffic rose, the inescapable essence of New York.

She drew the silk of her kimono around her shoulders, and studied the face in the mirror before her. The light brown hair, brushed sleekly back now and damp around the edges; the wide green eyes. The two inches of scar in front of her ear stood out red and ugly. She touched it with a fingertip, something she had only recently been able to do. It was still sore to pressure, but that hadn't been the reason for her unwillingness.

But it too was hers now, a part of her.

For the records, they had said. The implication had been that nobody would ever look at that hideous picture again, not that it would be available for casual viewing by everyone in the NYPD Data Control Center. At heart Catherine really didn't care. It was in the past.

She would, she thought, remembering back to those hellish twenty-four hours between her return and her entry to the hospital, have cared then, cared frenziedly, desperately. The hurt and the humiliation had been fresh, and it had seemed to her then that they would last undiminished for the remainder of her life. It was in her eyes in the picture: weary eyes, exhausted and bearing this only because she must.

It happened . . . and you're alive. What you endured will make you stronger.

How had he known?

She wanted to see him again, wanted to show him that he had been right. He would be glad, she knew, to see her whole, and strong, and happy. Wanted to touch his hand, to hear him talk about the world of the Tunnels, about his friends there, about his life. Wanted to tell him about the D.A.'s office, and Isaac; to talk over with him the startling and disconcerting revelations of learning how to fight, to hear what he had to say.

I know you, he had said. Sometimes she felt that he was the only one who truly did, or ever had.

She had been afraid, as the sticky and exhausting summer wore into fall, that he would grow dim to her, and the recollection of what it had been like to know him be gradually buried under the avalanche of new experience.

But he hadn't. At times it was enough for her to know that Vincent was there, living in the same city she did, in the same few square miles of ground; an awareness, like the awareness of the secret life flowing in the hive of Tunnels Below, which colored all her perceptions of the city and added another lamination of resonance to her world.

At times, it wasn't enough.

Her life these days was frenetic. It had been before, of course, but the uneasy round of parties, the late nights and tired mornings, had been of her own making, an escape from thoughts which had neither form nor possible conclusion. As she had told Edie that afternoon, they were still testing her—sometimes she was as surprised by the results of those tests as Moreno was—and she was still testing herself. Though she'd gradually become more confident about her abilities to do her job, and no longer grew depressed and miserable over not being able to deal single-handedly with the Augean Stables of the Justice Department, she would still come home trashed most nights, able to do little more than wash her face and fall into bed. It was days, she realized, since she'd had time to so much as phone her father. Or Tom, she added guiltily to herself. It had been days since she'd even *thought* about Tom. Yet every now and again, in times of quiet, it was as if she stopped and looked back on the road she had traveled . . . looked back, and looked around.

And in the rosy quiet of her room, at peace and doing no more than listening to the heartbeat of the city below, she was always aware that crowded as her days were, there was something that was missing from them: more than leisure, more than stillness, more than spiritual rest.

What was missing was Vincent.

Ten

"SHE can only bring you unhappiness!"

"Then I'll be unhappy." In the tawny shadows of his mane Vincent's eyes caught the gleam of the candles illuminating the study, reflective as a cat's. There was anger in them—not, Father thought, anger at him, but at Fate that had made him what he was, and at the world which was so constituted that he would inevitably be captured, locked away as a freak to be studied or killed outright by the fearful, should he be seen above the ground. This anger, dogged and bitter, was in every line of Vincent's powerful shoulders and back as he rose and paced, the brown leather-bound edition of *Great Expectations* still in his clawed hands.

He turned back, tall and feral in the molten light. "But I can't forget her. We're still connected."

Father was silent. He'd been afraid of that. Through summer and fall he'd been aware of Vincent's unhappiness, and knew that the woman Catherine was responsible; a rich man's daughter, like a woman he had himself once loved. If the rich were no more ruthless than the poor in the protection of their young, they were infinitely more powerful, a fact which he had once learned to his sorrow and which had kindled, in part, his fear surrounding the girl and his desire to get her out of the Tunnels as quickly as he could. Still, he remembered his pity for her, as he'd done what he could to close up the cuts on her ravaged face, and his rage at a world that could produce men who would do such a thing. It was that world, and all that it stood for, that he feared. For himself; for Vincent, his strange adopted son; for them all.

"I can feel what she feels," Vincent went on quietly. "I know what she's thinking, when she's frightened or happy or sad. She's a part of me."

And by the grief in his voice, Father knew it was more than that. "Vincent," he said, hurting with compassion for him, "your senses, your empathic powers, are quite extraordinary. It's your gift. And these powers have been heightened by the concern, by the love that you feel."

Vincent glanced around at him when he spoke the word *love*, understanding that he had guessed. There was a little silence, while the pipes spoke softly, the subway vibrated almost soundlessly overhead. Candles threw their diffuse shadows over the books heaped on tables and sideboards, across the marble faces of old statues and the arcane brass shapes of the antique instruments of medicine and navigation Father collected—the chewed refuse of a city that had neither time nor patience for past beauties, as it had neither time nor patience for such as they.

"But don't let your act of kindness destroy you." And it would destroy him, thought Father desperately, if it led him to forsake the Tunnels, even for a night, to go to her. Even if they didn't catch him—that nameless and terrible They who lived above—knowing he existed, they would begin to look, and the worst among them would be the most persistent in the search.

Looking at Vincent's face, Father could see that he knew all of this and more. But having known a great love himself, he could see also that Vincent, like one who discovers for the first time what light is, would be unable to forget it, or to be content with darkness. He knew the stuff of tragedy when he saw it, and his heart trembled.

Vincent sighed, set the book down on the study table, and turned to go. "Maybe I have no choice."

Mouse was waiting for him in the tunnels outside Father's rooms. "Vincent, need your help," he said in his light, quick voice, falling into step with his tall friend. "Help me?"

With Mouse, there was never any beating around the bush or subtle lead-ups. The smile that Vincent's face was ill-equipped to show quivered in his voice. "If I can."

"Can," affirmed Mouse confidently. He was a small, rather stocky youth of sixteen or seventeen, though nobody, least of all Mouse himself, was sure of his exact age. In a round, snub-nosed face beneath a pudding-bowl shock of sandy hair his blue eyes had a perpetually guileless expression completely at odds with his erratic intelligence, an intelligence that could analyze instinctively anything mechanical merely by looking at it, and, given even a modicum of tools and equipment, reproduce, repair, or improve it . . . if he considered doing so worth his time and energy, and wasn't off working on some other project at the time.

Where he'd come from nobody had the slightest

idea. Eight years ago Vincent had first become aware of him, a cautious shadow glimpsed in the Tunnels wherever there was food to be stolen, and for nearly eighteen months had patiently stalked the feral child like some giant cat through every far-flung cranny of the underground world. It had taken six men to finally corner the boy—screaming, biting, fighting in terror. But it was Vincent who had calmed him, tamed him; Vincent who, with infinite patience and care, had taught him to speak, and gradually brought him into the community of the Tunnelfolk.

Vincent's pains in that frustrating and maddening task had been well repaid. It was Mouse who had wired one or two areas of the Tunnels with emergency electricity if necessary, who had rigged systems to heat the water they drew from the city mains, who devised secret doors to guard the upper levels from chance incursions from Above. It was Mouse who understood where shortcuts could be made in the communication system of the pipes, who converted and reassembled devices to ease some of the endless hard labor of life below: a crude washing-machine system, improvements in fuels and stoves.

Unfortunately, Mouse was just as apt to expend his scattergun energies on pneumatic cookers that exploded and spattered food over a hundred square feet of tunnel roofs, on communication devices that embedded themselves in the walls with the speed and force of guided missiles, and refrigeration devices that blacked out twenty-five blocks of the city above. It was all one to him.

"Water pump in Old Main needs overhaul," he explained, pacing alongside Vincent and looking up at him with bright blue-gray eyes. "Pump's old, long haul to get water up to where people are. Pressure on main higher now ... don't know why.''

''Probably because the city's population has grown since it was first installed,'' mused Vincent.

Mouse shrugged with an extravagant spreading of his gloved hands. The city overhead interested him very little, except as a source of supply for his projects.

''Know where I can get parts to fix, parts to make better—everything. Pump twice as much water. Okay good—okay fine—but need help to get.''

Vincent halted, guessing what was coming next. ''And where are these parts?''

''Above!'' said Mouse with a wave of his arms, impatient at this display of obtuseness. ''Way out Nassau Street Line—good parts! Better than good! But need help. Three, four guys. Ask Father.''

Vincent tilted his head a little, regarding his friend in the shadowy glow of a kerosene lantern hanging on the rock wall nearby. His heart was still sore with the sense of hopelessness that had driven him to seek Father's company, but Mouse had a way of drawing anyone he came in contact with into his schemes. ''And what makes you think Father would approve if *I* asked, and not you?''

''You ask better,'' said Mouse brightly.

Vincent sighed. He had a feeling Mouse knew Father would not approve of this particular excursion, and he knew Mouse well enough to make an educated guess why not. Nevertheless, he promised, ''I'll speak to him tomorrow morning,'' and Mouse beamed.

''Good! Better than good.'' He cocked his head up at Vincent. ''You going walking?''

Vincent nodded.

"Want me along?"

Mouse, Vincent knew, would not have been in the slightest offended by a blunt no, as he never read into a rejection anything more than a temporary distaste for company. But he nodded, and the young man fell into step with him again as he prowled the Tunnels on his patrol. If one were suffering from a broken heart, Vincent supposed, it was at least an improvement to do so in the company of a friend.

Mouse enjoyed exploring the Tunnels as much as he did, and, alone among their denizens, knew them better. He was good company, too, sometimes talking of machines he had watched, with fascination, on his furtive journeys Above, or projects he was trying to assemble the parts to tinker together, sometimes prowling as silently as Vincent in his thick, cross-gaitered boots.

Few of the subterraneans were abroad at this time of night, for they tended for convenience to match the rhythms of their lives with those Above. The two friends prowled for a time down in the lower levels, below those places where the caverns were connected by old sewer lines and ancient steam-tunnels—isolated pockets of caves in places, or twisting skeins of tunnels in the bedrock. Here and there they came across the gates and warning signs posted to keep the children—and the less Tunnelwise adults—out of the more dangerous areas. Vincent knew he hadn't regarded them as a child, and sometimes wondered uneasily if other children were as confident of their abilities as he had been.

But when they ascended to the metal door that gave onto the drainage culvert in Central Park,

Mouse bade him good-night. Mouse had no use for fresh air; landscapes composed entirely of grass and trees bored him. "Grass is grass," he argued, as Vincent reached up into the junction box and tripped the lever that opened the sheet-steel door. Behind it was a rusted gate of iron bars that gave unwillingly to his shoulder. "Trees is trees. Tunnels . . ." His blue eyes softened a little with one of the few expressions of aesthetic appreciation Vincent had seen in his friend. "Tunnels always different, always new."

Vincent's eyes smiled, and he raised the hood of his cloak to cover his face. "'To see a world in a grain of sand,'" he quoted softly, "'and Heaven in a wild flower.'"

Mouse gestured impatiently. "Wet grass!" And with a grin he was gone.

To hold Infinity in the palm of your hand, Vincent finished to himself as he stepped out into the thick-scented darkness of the muggy night, *and Eternity in an hour.*

Hot and dank as it was, the night was an intoxication. At this hour the park was deserted, and in any case Vincent's night-sighted eyes and acute hearing, trained even more sharply by the limited sensations of the Tunnels, would warn him of anyone's approach long before he himself might be seen, and enable him to seek shelter in the blackness beneath the trees. Father, he knew, did not approve of these nocturnal rambles, but would not forbid them. They were his only chance to touch, however briefly, the world that could never be his. From everything he had heard of it, from the newspapers and books he had read, from those who had fled it to seek sanctuary below, he wasn't altogether certain he would want to be a part of it even if he could. But previously his regrets had been confined to a certain sorrow that he would never be able to enter the echoing gray vaults of Notre Dame de Paris, or see a play any more complex than the small productions gotten up for Winterfest celebrations, or swim in the ocean.

All that had changed.

From the woods at the edge of the Ramble he could see the building where she lived. Mouse could pinpoint any address in the five boroughs from the steam-tunnels that ran beneath, but Vincent, scarcely less adept at this, could in addition correlate Above and Below. His ability to locate any point in the city and get there, sometimes literally in minutes if the subways were running right, was uncanny.

That corner terrace, where apricot light softly outlined a window, a pair of small-paned French doors . . . Looking across at it, he knew instinctively it was hers.

Why do this to himself? he wondered. Father was undoubtedly right. Except that there was no way that she would ever bring him unhappiness . . . or at least the unhappiness would never counterbalance the joy of having known her.

His mind sorted the cadences of Donne, finding in their resonances the echo of his own strange ache.

I wonder, by my troth, what thou and I
Did til we loved? Were we not weaned til then?

No, he thought. He had understood that his life in the world Below was incomplete, as he had long ago accepted that it must be, but he saw now that like a child—like the lovers of Donne's poem—he had been missing some component of reality of whose very existence he had hitherto been ignorant.

And no matter how much it hurt, it was an ignorance to which he could not, and did not want to, return.

If ever any beauty I did see,
Which I desired, and got, 'twas but a dream of thee.

Above that white terrace balustrade, the light went out. She slept, then. He turned away, and hoped her dreams were dreams of peace.

"Mouse, it's out of the question," sighed Father, in the resigned tone of voice Vincent had frequently heard in the old man's dealing with Mouse. "I've told you before there is no way I can countenance your stealing."

"Not *stealing*," argued Mouse, with a frustrated gesture—he'd had this argument with Father before. "*Taking*."

"'Taking' from where?"

"Above." The wave of his hand amply indicated that for Mouse, the world of daylight outside the Tunnels was one gigantic dumpster filled with pickings. Winslow, sitting on the curving granite steps of Father's loft between Mary and Pascal, rolled his eyes. He too had tried before to argue semantics with Mouse. Mouse went on eagerly, "Good place, big building filled with stuff; cables, motors, pipe. Don't have to pick apart pieces, file new teeth, clean off grease." Mouse frowned, trying as he often did to make Father understand. "Stealing from *people*. This just . . . taking."

Father sighed, and rubbed the inner corners of his eyes.

Vincent, true to his promise, had put to Father Mouse's proposal for a scavenging expedition for parts to fix the Old Main pump, adding noncommittally that Mouse had requested three or four men to help him carry the equipment. That in itself was a dead giveaway, not that there had been any doubt in either his or Father's minds. Usually it took half a dozen small, furtive trips all over the city to assemble the requisite pieces for any complicated machine Mouse or Winslow proposed to tinker together. Because of the importance of the pump a half dozen of the adults of the community had been called together for an informal conference, but the result was a foregone conclusion.

"No."

"That pump's pretty damn old," put in Winslow, leaning forward on his elbows. "I think Mouse is right; something has to be done about it. The motor's lugging bad, and if it quits not only are we gonna have to be toting water up here by hand, but the pressure on that main's gonna build up pretty bad. We're probably gonna have leakage through that whole area."

Father frowned. "How's that?"

"The main's one of the oldest in the city," explained Pascal, with a gesture of his shabbily gloved hands. It was unusual for him to be out of the pipe chamber, but in this case his opinion as the most senior member of the community, the one who had dwelled there the longest, since his birth, had been necessary. In his absence from the pipe chamber the knockings and tappings hadn't stopped; rather, they had multiplied, communications being less efficient without him.

"Parts of it must date back to Aaron Burr's time," he went on. "That particular pump's been there for as long as I've been around, bleeding off city water, and it's kept the p.s.i. on that main from getting too high even though the volume of water in general has increased." He paused a moment as tapping sounded on the pipes, subconsciously tilting his head to listen. "Excuse me."

He got quickly to his feet, climbed the few stairs to the floor of the loft, and picked his way through the piles of books to the pipes that ran up the wall. Taking a small crescent-wrench from an inner pocket of his voluminous green mantle he tapped a flurry of coded words on the pipe, paused to listen for a moment, then returned to his seat. "I'm sorry . . . One of the Helpers was trying to contact Sara in the candle shop and had the wrong pipe. If the pump goes out the water pressure will build . . ."

"Is there a danger of flooding?" asked Father quickly. "The Old Main isn't that far beneath the lower portions of the inhabited tunnels." Sitting just beneath the staircase Ho and two of the older girls who were also Mouse's friends—Jamie and Laura—glanced worriedly at one another in the flickering glow of the candles.

Pascal frowned, and looked inquiringly at Winslow, who shook his head noncommittally. "The last time it went out, when I was a kid, it got kind of gooey down there," he said slowly. "A lot of mud—it was a mess to clean up—but nothing catastrophic. But with the higher pressure in the mains these days, frankly, I don't know."

Father turned back to Mouse. "Can you get us a parts list, Mouse?" he asked. "An idea of what you'd need to repair the pump?"

137

Mouse nodded emphatically. "Four guys." He thought about it a moment more, then amplified, "With sacks. Need sacks to carry stuff."

Father turned to the others. "We can put out word among the Helpers; see what can be found, or raised piecemeal by legal means. Is this acceptable?"

"It's slow," pointed out Winslow, folding his big, callused hands over his patched knees. "That main's one of the major sources of water. We're gonna be hauling a lot of buckets if the pump quits."

"Is it in immediate danger of doing so?"

The blacksmith thought about it for a moment, then shook his head. "Not in my opinion, no. But it's close to it, and you never can tell when a machine that old will give up."

"And the Helpers can only give us so much," added Mary quietly, from her perch beside Winslow's feet. "Food and blankets, thread and medicines and fuel are one thing. Machinery is another. It's expensive, and it may take time. But at the moment I can't think of another way."

As the members of the informal council were leaving the study Ho paused, and lingered when Mouse, Laura, and Jamie walked together out into the dark. Then she came back to where Father still sat at his desk, Vincent standing quietly at his side.

"Father," she said quietly, "I don't want to sound impertinent, but . . . why not do it Mouse's way?"

"Because," said Father gently, "we are not a community of thieves."

"Well, from what Mouse has told me it sounds like the place he has in mind is a kind of a salvage yard out in Brooklyn. It's not like the stuff was new, or he was getting it from a store or anything.''

"He would still be taking what belongs to someone else, what someone else had paid for, even at scrap yard prices," pointed out Father. "He would still be taking something that someone else could make a living from."

Her lips tightened, and a gleam of resentment flickered in her black almond eyes. "Do we owe them that kind of hairsplitting?" With a slight jerk of her head she motioned upwards, to the room's vaulted stone ceiling, and, through the granite above, to the city, its people, the world they had left behind them.

Father folded his hands, and looked up at the thin girl in her bulky sweater, her vest cut of quilted cotton moving-pads, her patched and baggy jeans. "We owe it to ourselves," he said. "Thievery has a tendency to escalate, Ho, as indeed any vice does. What starts as a little ends in dangerous excess."

Her bony figure shifted, as if trying to sidestep what he said. "I know that," she said uncomfortably. "But we need that stuff. You know as well as I do most of the Helpers are people who don't have a lot to give. They can't take the time to go scrounging around looking for six three-eighths-inch couplings or fifteen feet of three-quarters-inch brass pipe or whatever. Half the stuff they'll get for us won't be any good. It never is. If that pump bites it before Mouse can get it fixed, I for one ain't looking forward to carrying buckets up to take a bath."

Father shook his head. "Neither are any of us. And we'll all be taking a turn until something else can be rigged."

"So why can't we just . . . It *is* kind of an emergency."

The old man sighed. "An emergency can be a very forceful excuse, but it is an excuse nonetheless, and excuses tend to diminish in urgency as time goes by. We can't do it, Ho. Our world is a very fragile place, and we inhabit it under certain conditions. But we can't use those conditions—the secrecy that shelters us, the Helpers who conceal us, the Tunnels that let us come and go unseen by those Above—to violate the rules by which we live."

His glance went to Vincent, standing silently at his side, and Vincent knew that it was to him, as much as to Ho, that he added, "We are of this world. We cannot have it both ways."

The girl hunched her shoulders, but nodded unwillingly. "All right," she said, and turning, walked from the room.

"It's hard for her," said Vincent quietly, when she had gone.

His father regarded him quietly, steadily, for a moment, then sighed, and wearily rubbed his eyes. "It's hard for us all."

Eleven

It was still dark when Catherine climbed the steps of police headquarters, slick with last night's rain, though at this hour the leading edge of the morning rush hour was already jamming the streets. Park Row, pointing northeast toward the river, was a wind tunnel specifically designed to channel the bitter December blasts.

I must be crazy, she thought, huddling her bright-colored duffle coat nearer around her. A year ago she hadn't even known there *was* such a thing as six in the morning. *But, dammit, if I don't do this now, when will I get the chance? The meeting with Moreno about the Winthrop appeal is at four and it'll run well past seven, and if those reports are going to get in on the Bajeer case I'm going to be at my desk through lunch . . . again.*

She sighed and shook her head as she rode up the elevator to Data Control. No wonder Joe lived on cheese puffs and candy bars—it was the only food you could count on around here.

To her eyes, still gritty from slightly too little sleep, the eternal white fluorescence of the computer room had a tawdriness, like a restaurant after hours when all the lights are up and the dirt shows. Without its bustling crowd of programmers and analysts it echoed. Here and there a solitary figure pecked at a terminal, or slouched blearily over *The Times* and a doughnut, not even raising their heads as Catherine threaded her way between the cubicles. Bits of tinsel hung on some cubicle partitions, Christmas cards decorated others—someone had put up a huge blue-and-white Mogen David on a bulletin board. There would be a party, Catherine knew, Christmas day—a holiday swapped into by most of the Jews and Moslems of the division in trade for Passover and Ramadan—but the NYPD wouldn't close.

She had waked last night in a curiously restive mood, her mind jigglingly alert with the sensation of something forgotten, something important. She had a sense of having dreamed something . . . Yes.

She'd dreamed about Captain Hermann.

She'd been thumbing through a report at her desk, and he'd been sitting across from her, he and Tom. She'd looked up at them, and had said, "What do you mean, *inactive?* You can't close this file." The report, she had realized, was about her own assault.

Hermann, big and ruddy-faced and rumpled as ever, had shrugged. "What can you do, when the girl wouldn't tell me anything? She's got to have been lying."

"Of course she was lying," returned Tom indignantly, his brown eyes hard. "*I* know they raped her, they have to have. It was her own fault—she should have stuck with me like I told her to, instead of walking out. She should have done what I told her to. And frankly, I think she should have told us about that, so we could get this thing

142

straightened out and things can go back to being the way they were. But she won't say anything."

And then Catherine herself had been sitting on the other side of the desk. From across the desk Catherine looked at that battered, dirty girl in her torn black dress, her sutured nightmare of a face; met her own green eyes. She had said gently to herself, "What happened?"

"I don't want to talk about it," that other Catherine said. "I don't want to think about it, don't want to go through it again. It wasn't my fault. It was nobody's fault. It was just one of those things."

"No," said Catherine quietly. "There's no such thing as 'just one of those things.'"

The battered girl had not replied, but tears had welled in the swollen eyes. Catherine had looked down at the report in front of her, filling it in for her, so she wouldn't have to take that other self, that hurt and broken self, through the pain of reliving what was, to her, a black and personal nightmare. She wanted to tell her, wanted to reassure her, that the pain would not last, the horror would not last, but knew, having been there herself, that she would not believe it.

Instead she concentrated on filling in the gaps in the report, her own neat handwriting picking up where Hermann's scrawl had left off. Captain Hermann, she noted—as she had noted when in waking reality she had actually seen the file—filled in his reports even more hastily and sloppily than she did.

The three men were waiting in the alley with a van. The first man said, "Goin' home alone tonight, Carol?"

She frowned as she wrote the words. She hadn't remembered anything much after, "Goin' home alone." Only a nightmare of pain and terror, a terror she would rather not revisit, locked and sealed behind the black doors of her mind.

But they had said, "Carol."

And as if that other Catherine, the girl sitting huddled on the other side of her desk, were dictating, Catherine wrote, *Stocky man said something about, "Little girls with big mouths." This argues that the assault was a planned hit, rather than random violence or vengeance in a personal matter. Course of suggested action . . .*

And then her eyes had opened, and she had stared for a long time at the soft pattern of squares of reflected streetlights thrown through the French doors onto her bedroom ceiling, until the sky outside had begun to pale with false dawn.

Edie was at the BIF station, so absorbed in the program she was checking that she didn't look up until Catherine was almost beside her. Then she grinned, her mobile face miming astonishment. "Well, what are *you* doin' here at six A.M., girlfren'? Just gittin' home from the discos?"

There was no animosity in her voice now, and Catherine laughed. These days when Edie gave her a hard time about being an uptown rich girl, or a bleeding-heart liberal, it was because they both knew the accusations weren't true. Catherine slipped out of her coat. "God, I can't *remember* the last time I was in a disco."

"Tell me about it." Edie tapped in a shutdown as Catherine took the chair next to the table containing a secondary system, a printer, a 2400-baud modem, a fax machine, and a red stoneware cup of faintly steaming tea. The operator heaved a mock sigh, and patted the terminal fondly. "You know Biff here is the longest relationship I've had since the sixth grade. Biff understands me."

Catherine nodded judiciously. "Could be the wave of the future."

Lately Edie had begun to instruct her in the mysteries of computers, whenever their fragments of spare time coincided; thanks to her, Catherine, though still computer-ignorant, was no longer under the subconscious impression that computers were plotting to take over the world. "Hell," Edie had said over coffee at Tummy Time on another hideously early morning, "it's more a case of the right hand not knowin' what the left hand is doin', raised up to powers of ten. You ever try to line up one file with another from a system that ain't compatible?"

"Listen," said Catherine, after they'd traded shop gossip a little and bemoaned the frenziedness of their respective lives, "I need some help, and it's a little tricky. A woman was attacked by mistake . . . by three men. I want to find out if these men ever went after their intended victim."

Edie turned back to the screen. There was nothing, Catherine knew, that Edie liked better than to "thumb through the mainframe," as she termed it, sifting through files and finding new ways to play with these marvelous toys. "Got the date of the mistaken attack?"

"Last April twelfth," said Catherine without hesitation, and Edie, intent as she was on calling up her program, caught some note in her voice that made her turn.

After a moment's pause she asked, "Aggravated assault?"

Catherine nodded.

Pale blue on dark, the screen filled itself with

lines of names, each appended with the date of April 12, then casually scrolled down for a second screenful, a third . . .

"Lot of guys hittin' on a lot of women out there," said Edie, her voice dry. Catherine thought she'd glimpsed her own name on the list, up on the first screen with the rest of the *C*'s, but wasn't sure. "Can we narrow this down? Domestic, in the street . . . ?"

"In a van," said Catherine slowly, remembering how the lights had come up in the misty darkness of the alley behind her. Or was that only the recollection of her dream? That awful dream of running in slow motion, unable to get away. "I don't know what make."

If the programmer thought anything, or guessed anything, of the hesitancy in her voice she made no comment. All she said was, "How 'bout the intended victim's name?"

Goin' home alone tonight, Carol? And the terrible iron strength of the hand around her waist. She remembered it all, now.

My name isn't Carol, she'd gasped, pleaded. They hadn't listened.

"Try Carol."

The smooth oval of her lips pressed taut, Edie factored in the new data. "Okay, here are the Carols. Let's punch it to the files."

The first Carol attacked on April 12 was sixty-three years old. Even five months in the D.A.'s office hadn't accustomed Catherine to that.

"Let's try the next," she said, keeping the rage out of her voice. (*You can't fix it all.*) "It would be a woman in her twenties or thirties."

146

VICTIM NAME—FELWAY, CAROL

DATE OF INCIDENT—12 APRIL 1986

HAIR—BLACK, EYES—BROWN

HT—5'7", WT—144

SEX—FEMALE, DOB 17 MAY 1964

STATUS—UNDER INVESTIGATION

FILE NO—ADRX 73856

Then a brief blur of grays and blacks, and the digitalized picture (*For the records* ... Catherine could still hear the police saying it as the flashbulb went off in her aching eyes) of a young black woman with a swollen jaw.

"No," she said softly. "Try the next."

VICTIM NAME—STABLER, CAROL

DATE OF INCIDENT—12 APRIL 1986

HAIR—LIGHT BROWN, EYES—GREEN

HT—5'5", WT—105

SEX—FEMALE, DOB 05 FEB 1960

STATUS—NOT IN CUSTODY

FILE NO—ADRX 78315

Despite the bruises and lacerations—and she had been very seriously beaten indeed—the resemblance of the girl in the picture to Catherine was eerie. Catherine closed her eyes as a wave of some emotion she would be hard put to define washed over her. She had known it had to be so, but evidently knowing it and actually seeing this other woman's face, like some appalling mirror of her own, were different matters.

Then the anger came back, anger and the chill, businesslike knowledge that there was, in fact, something she could do about it. "This could be it," she said, looking back at Edie, and saw in the other woman's eyes recognition and dawning knowledge. "Let's pull the file."

The address in Carol Stabler's file was on West 28th Street not far from Madison Square Garden, a shabby apartment building whose beige-painted hallways smelled vaguely of uncleaned carpets and of somebody cooking spaghetti. At this hour of the evening the tinny whisper of television sets behind every one of those shut brown doors was ubiquitous; somewhere a baby screamed on, uncomforted.

Catherine found the door and knocked, and received no answer. There was no TV on inside, but music instead, a woman's sweet voice with a lyric country twang. The song finished and another began . . . not radio, then, but a record. That meant someone was home.

She knocked again.

"Who is it?" The voice through the door sounded scared.

"Carol?" It felt odd to call out to someone she had never met. She could almost sense her, standing close to the door, that fair-haired woman who could so easily be mistaken for herself on a dark street, in the shadows away from the hotel's lights.

The voice was louder, with brittle bravado. "What do you want?"

"My name's Cathy Chandler. I'd like to talk to you."

There was a long hesitation. Horribly, Catherine remembered the old *Saturday Night Live* gag of the Land Shark: "It's a candygram . . . It's the plumber . . . It's flowers . . ." She wondered how the men had found Carol, how they had lured her someplace where they could get hold of her. The Boston Strangler, she remembered, had usually said he was a plumber, to get his victims to open the door.

In her report to the police, Carol had refused to say.

There was the snick and rattle of deadbolts going over. There were two. One, Catherine could see from looking at the door, was a couple of years old, the other new. Since April, she thought. She understood the feeling. The first month or so she'd had to talk herself out of barricading her doors every night.

Then the door opened a chained crack, and through the few inches of space a pair of frightened green eyes looked out.

Like Catherine, she had once been very beautiful. At the time of the assault her file had listed her occupation as "Actress"—not that that meant anything, in New York—but Catherine doubted she even kept up the pretense of it, these days. She had evidently not been slashed, but her left eyelid drooped flaccidly over the eye, and the whole left side of her face had the curious dead immobility of nerve damage. Catherine shivered. She realized only then how much she truly had to thank her father for.

Carol's voice was hard, braver now that she saw

Catherine was by herself. "What's this about? You a cop?"

"I'm with the district attorney's office."

She held out her card to the other woman, but Carol pushed it angrily back at her. "Look, I told you people to leave me alone!" Her voice was shaky with fear that bordered on hysteria. "You caused me enough trouble, I got nuthin' to say." She pulled her head back and started to close the door. Almost instinctively Catherine put out a hand, bracing it against the grimy panels.

"Carol, you're not the only one they hurt!"

For a moment the pressure on the door was wholehearted. Then it slacked. Carol's thin, half-paralyzed face, framed in a soft wisp of hair the identical shade of Catherine's dark, dusty blonde, reappeared around the edge of the wood.

"What're you talking about?"

"They got you and me mixed up." She stepped closer, into the bar of yellow light that fell through the slot of the chained door, and brushed back the hair that usually fell forward, framing her face and hiding the scar. Even with makeup covering it, the mark was still glaringly visible at close range.

"Carol, I think this was meant for you."

Carol's slim hand flew to cover her mouth, to hide its sudden tremor as she stared. For a moment she said nothing, made no sound, only looked. Then, her voice breaking with fury and denial, she cried, "*Go away!*"

She shoved the door to. Catherine could hear the locks slamming over on the other side, and above them, Carol's muffled sobs.

By the birthdate in her file Carol would be, what? Twenty-two? Twenty-three? The file had mentioned no family in New York, no regular boyfriend, and

Catherine had gotten from it no sense of anyone close enough to Carol to have helped her through that. Not even a doctor. She thought of her own days of misery and pain and terror after the assault, of Vincent's quiet, steady voice, of her father's unquestioning support through the long days of her recuperation after the facial surgery. According to the file, Carol had had her bruises treated in the Emergency Room at NYU Medical Center, and had gone home.

Home to nothing but the fear that it could happen again.

Even after eight months it was clear that the fear was very much alive.

After a long moment Catherine stooped, to slide her card under the door. "If you want to talk to somebody who understands how you feel," she said quietly, pitching her voice to carry through the door, "call me."

There was no reply but the sound of sobbing, as if the woman were leaning against the door, locked and barred and chained like a prison's, unable for the moment to turn back into her apartment, weeping her heart out.

Hurting for her, Catherine walked away down the hall.

Iron arms locked around her; terrible strength lifted her off her feet. She struggled, fought, kicked, panting with exertion, and a man's voice whispered hot and thick in her ear, "You can't do nuthin', can you? You better do somethin'."

Cold gray January light filled the loft. Desperately, Catherine struggled to break Isaac's grip, which pinned her arms, dropping her weight against his, wriggling, trying to drive in her elbows against the hard ridges of the protective padding he wore over chest and belly and groin. In spite of the sweatband around her forehead her hair tangled in her mouth and eyes. He was using his full strength to hold her, as an assailant would, and he was terrifyingly strong.

"Whaddaya gonna do?" he taunted her, his unshaven lips bristly against her ear around the edge of the face-guard he wore. "C'mon, whaddaya gonna do?"

For a moment despair tugged at her, and she wanted to stop and ask *What CAN I do?* He was bigger than she, taller and heavier; he had a man's strength. But some instinct within her told her that this time, he wouldn't stop. *Dammit*, she thought, *it isn't fair, I'm not ready*.

She hadn't been ready for the men in the van, either.

That thought brought others; the memory of their strength, and the hideous, kinesthetic recollection of her helplessness against them. It was more than remembering. She was back in that night, smelling the rain and exhaust and steam, smelling the man's sweat and hair oil, back on the sidewalk with the van's door slamming open in front of her. Back helpless, back scared, knowing what was going to happen next—like that other girl in her dream, huddled in her torn dress, whispering, "Just one of those things."

The shell she'd built around those memories cracked. The wall she'd put them behind to protect her from their intensities, to protect her from the fear, split open with a sensation almost palpable in her chest, and the raw blackness of the fear boiled forth, transmuted to killing rage.

With a cry like an animal's she got her toe

hooked around Isaac's knee, jerking and twisting. The joint gave, and as her other foot touched the floor she thrust back against him with all her strength. Taken off-balance the black man fell backwards, and Catherine, using her body as a weapon, slammed down on top of him, twisting sharply as his grip loosened when they hit the mat. With a scream she didn't realize she'd uttered, she was on her feet, kicking him from her with all her strength as he tried to get up and come at her, kicking him again as he was down. Something like fire kindled in the pit of her being, blazed up to ignite her flesh. She grabbed for the nearest weapon, a baseball bat they'd been using at their last lesson three days ago; he was starting to get up again.

Any man, any man who laid hands on her, once she got him down was not going to get up again . . .

"Stop!"

For one split second there was genuine fear in his voice.

She stopped as if he'd hit her between the eyes.

The baseball bat was upraised in her hands. Her throat was raw and sore— Had she cried out? Broken her eternal low-voiced, well-bred soft-spokenness? Her arms hurt where she'd wrenched them against his, her hair tangled over her eyes like a crazy woman's, her gray sweatclothes were splotched with perspiration and her body still stinging from the impact with the floor.

For an instant Isaac looked up at her with startled, bemused eyes. "Was that *you?*" He half laughed, like a man just off a roller coaster—or perhaps it was because he saw in that taut, furious form before him the well-dressed young lady who had come to him that fall in her high heels and Ann Taylor suit. "That really you?"

She lowered the bat. She was winded, panting, but every atom of her flesh glowed. Like him, she felt as if she'd just come off a roller coaster. She wanted to say, *I guess so*, but couldn't—and anyway she wasn't sure it *was* her.

She could only laugh, in exhilaration and triumph.

Twelve

It was his dreams that woke Vincent, long before Pascal began to sound the alarm on the pipes.

They were dreams of darkness, thick-laden with a sense of peril. *Water*, he thought. Deep water, rushing fast and cold through black rock-seams, dashing itself against the hewed walls, water bubbling around the iron staples in the ladder-wells, swirling over brick steps. With his queer, colorless night-vision he saw it spraying from cracks and fissures in the curved wall of a great gray pipe—surely the Old Main that ran just below the lowest levels of habitation?—pouring from the ruptured joints of a dozen connecting lines, bubbling out into the surrounding soil as, once the pump quit and the pressure built to intolerable levels, the Old Main gave at every point of its length.

His eyes opened to near-total darkness. Usually dim illumination leaked at all times through the big fan-shaped window of apricot stained glass which looked out onto the Long Chamber, a sort of rectangular common-room where half a dozen of the main inhabited tunnels came together. It was lit at all times with kerosene and candlelight, but now the glow was jittery, thready, frantic, as people seized any light they could.

He was up and pulling on shirt and breeches in the gloom when the alarm began to clang over the pipes: *MAYDAY, MAYDAY, MAYDAY! Flooding—red alert—flooding—prepare to evacuate* . . . a wild and frenzied clamor, like Poe's poetry, which echoed and reechoed in his mind . . .

> (*Hear the loud alarum bells,*
> *Brazen bells!*
> *What a tale of terror now their*
> *turbulency tells!* . . .)

Vincent could move cat-fast when he wanted to; his boots were on and he was up the steps and in the Long Chamber beyond before the first of the message was done.

He knew already that the flood was down in the tunnels connecting with the Old Main.

"Told you so! Told you so!" Mouse was gasping to the little group of men and women at the top of the long Circular Stair that led to the lower portions of the inhabited area of the Tunnels. Some of them—Father and Winslow, disheveled and half-dressed—held lanterns. Mouse had a sodium-bulb flashlight whose hard blue glare outlined their faces in shadow and gleamed on the heaving black water visible far down the shaft of the stair. "Pump stopped—pressure in the main built up."

"I didn't think the pressure'd go that high," said Winslow. "It musta burst all along the old section."

"How far can it spread?" demanded Father. "How far up do you think it can come?" Over the years he had been putting together a series of maps of the world below the ground, whose caverns and tunnels were far from contiguous, but even with the help of such experts as Vincent and Mouse they were far from complete. Besides, Mouse had a tendency to forget to tell him about all the passages and tunnels he knew.

"I don't know," said Winslow. "Up as high as the Brick Steps for sure."

"Have the people who live down that far been evacuated?"

"Some," said Mary, coming up quickly behind him with a lamp in her hand. "Some were cut off by the flooded sections."

"Ho lives down there!" gasped Luke, crowding up behind them. "She has one of the deepest rooms, near the South Pockets . . . My God!" With an abrupt movement he turned, beginning to tear off his old green blanket-coat, and Vincent and Father caught him by the arms.

"Don't be a fool, man," said Father, and the young man stopped struggling and stared at him, his broad face pale with shock. Father turned to Vincent and Mouse. "Is there any way out of there besides the stairs?"

"Vent shaft," said Mouse promptly, and his expressive hands sketched a square about ten inches across. "Too small to crawl."

A swift staccato clanged on the pipes that ran along the wall, and Father tilted his head to listen, the others falling silent around him. *Bernardo and Zena evacuated safe . . . Sarah, Dustin, Quinn trapped.*

"Damn," whispered Father desperately.

"There's a roof-chamber above the third room over from the candle-room," said Vincent quickly.

"If they're cut off they should at least be safe there from the rising water."

Father glanced queryingly at Mouse, who nodded decisively and said, "Okay fine." Mary turned at once and, pulling a long-barreled key from her pocket, began rapping out the message on the nearest pipe: *Third chamber down, roof-chamber safe . . .*

"What about Regan and her children?" asked Father, looking over at Mary again. "They live in one of the lower rooms and we haven't heard from them. They might have been cut off by the flood and forced back into the South Pockets."

"There's no way out of the South Pockets," pointed out Vincent worriedly.

"I'm not sure Regan knows that. There are a lot of passages in there; if the flood was coming in from one direction she might take a chance."

Vincent turned his head, looked down the vast open well of the Circular Stair to the doorway that led into the lower areas of habitation, half-submerged in the lapping black water. Luke caught his arm, looking up at him pleadingly. "Ho's down there . . ." the young man whispered, and Vincent reviewed in his mind the corridors and turnings of that area, where Regan and her children lived and the rather isolated passageway beyond where Ho had made her home. Floor-level there dipped and varied. Some of it would be completely submerged by this time. If Regan and her children had been driven back that way by the floodwaters . . .

"It seems I must," he said, and began to unlace his boots.

There was another urgent tattoo on the pipes, as Pascal collected maydays in the Pipe Chamber, relayed information about routes still open for evacuation, about who had reported in and who had not. Vincent had a vivid mental picture of the little man, as he'd so often seen him in the gloom and candlelight of that enormous cavern, wielding a pair of wrenches like drumsticks against the tangled spiderweb of iron all around him.

Laura in South Pockets, the message said. *Water up the Brick Steps. Quicksand.*

"If the Brick Steps are flooded it means the water's coming around the other side as well," said Father softly. "That means that section over near the Stone Bridge where Benjamin lives may need to be evacuated."

"Pipe-tunnel two chambers over," provided Mouse. "Ladder up—quicksand pockets all over there, though."

Vincent looked down into the lightless well of the air-shaft and thought about negotiating the mazes of the South Pockets in the dark. "Mouse," he said quietly, "unless you're needed elsewhere, could you go to the Pipe Chamber with Pascal? I may need directions once I'm down."

"Okay fine," said the little man, and, setting down his lamp, went bolting away into the darkness.

Someone in the little group around the stair-head produced a rope. Vincent tied it in a quick slip-knot around the back of his belt, firm but easy to release in case it fouled. "Play it out steadily," he instructed Luke, who was gathering the coils around his arm. "Parts of the corridor may be underwater by the time we're coming out. We'll need a guide."

Luke nodded shakily, having accepted the fact that others were more qualified than he to rescue the woman he loved. Vincent started down the steps, the chipped and pitted limestone icy under his bare feet. The Stair, like so many of the other structures of the Tunnels, was ancient, built long ago by God know who. It made a long, swooping helix around an open darkness in the center of the shaft, and from that darkness came the sinister lap of the sour waters. Above him he heard Father's voice, firing rapid orders about rescue and evacuation operations, and above it all the pipes clashed, high and urgent and brazen.

Mayday—prepare evacuation all chambers near Stone Bridge—all stand ready . . .

> *(Yet the ear it fully knows,*
> *By the twanging,*
> *And the clanging,*
> *How the danger ebbs and flows . . .)*

He descended into darkness.

The doorway into the lower inhabited corridors, with its incongruously carved pediment of Apollo and the Graces, salvaged from some long-forgotten Bleecker Street mansion, was submerged at the level of Vincent's breast. A strong current surged inwards, dragging at his linen shirt where it stuck to his shoulders and back, and on it drifted small household objects: two or three baskets, an old crate of the kind children went on their food-gathering expeditions with, a straw fan, a monkey-pod bowl. This area was the lower extent of the inhabited portion of the Tunnels, but perhaps a dozen families and groups lived down here, separated only by a relatively short distance from the rest of the community above.

Farther on lay Ho's rooms, somewhat isolated— though not nearly as distant as those of such free spirits as Mouse and Narcissa—and, beyond them, the South Pockets, a system of natural caves which, like this portion of the tunnels, had been partially excavated and added to at some time in the city's history, by whom or for what purposes no one remembered. There were a number of such mysterious excavations beneath New York, systems of tunnels below the usual level of even the deepest sub-basements. Some of them, like the intricate network of stairways and mazes below Chinatown, had been partially abandoned by those who dug them and taken over later by the Tunnel dwellers, though at least one such system, under a tailor shop in the East Forties, was still in active use by what Father guessed to be a clandestine government agency—it was one of Mouse's best sources of pilfered electricity. In other places it was simply a matter of shafts having been sunk from the sub-basements of Park Avenue mansions now long torn down and replaced by blocks of apartments, some of them the small chambers that had housed elevator shafts, others secret rooms carved from the rock for reasons long forgotten, or ancient smuggler-tunnels dating back to the days of the Revolution and before.

The tunnel turned. Floor and ceiling dipped, the water level now covering Vincent's shoulders, lifting the ends of his long hair. Even with the downturn of the floor at this point, the water shouldn't have been this deep. The level was still rising. By the time he came back, he thought, glancing behind him at the narrow rectangle of clear air at the top of the door, the passage might well be completely filled.

He looked ahead, to where the roof met the bobbing black surface of the flood. It was a swim of about sixty feet to the crossing-seam that joined with the shaft up into Ho's rooms, and once he made the corner, about thirty beyond that. The crosscut was the second on the right—he'd have to keep one hand on the wall.

Carefully, he drew on the cable floating behind him until he had seventy or eighty feet of slack. The risk of getting fouled in it was less than that of Luke's not playing it fast enough once he started swimming, and holding him back.

He swam forward cautiously, keeping contact with the right-hand wall, the ceiling lowering steadily over his head. In twenty feet he'd reached the end of the airspace. It was less than he'd thought. The level was still going up.

Taking a deep breath, he plunged.

Striking forward in absolute blackness, it was difficult to estimate distances. He'd either missed the first cross-tunnel or his judgment of how long he'd been under was completely out. He slid forward through the sightless water like a shark, fast and efficient, his hand feeling the rock wall . . . Too long, he had to have passed the first turning. When the wall dropped back beneath his fingertips he turned, remembering uncomfortably that the first tunnel went downwards after fifty feet. If he'd miscalculated it would be far too late to turn back and try again. His lungs were aching already.

He struck upwards, and his head touched the ceiling. He gave another kick, driving his body forward, then felt the upper edge of a rising shaft brush against his hair, and kicked again, plowing upwards. His head cleared water, and opening his eyes he saw the dim flicker of reflected firelight at the top of the shaft. Somewhere in the darkness there came the desperate clatter of the pipes.

"Ho!" he called out, treading water for a moment to catch his breath. "Regan, Laura . . . !"

But only silence met him.

Above him and to his right a tenuous glimmer of reflected candlelight outlined the rectangle of a doorway. He guessed rather than saw the metal staples of a ladder leading down from it, and struck out across the well of the shaft. The door was some fifteen feet up; he carefully drew on the guiding cable until he had enough to reach, then climbed, detaching the line from his belt and tying it to the topmost rung. If he couldn't find those who had taken refuge in the Pockets and get them back here by the time the water rose that far, he reflected, they would all be in more trouble than they could get out of in any case.

Wiping himself down to get rid of the water, he padded down the short, brick-paved hall toward the light.

The light, as he'd suspected, came from Ho's room. Generally when children came down from Above—screened for trustworthiness by the Council, even as the adults were, though more allowances were made—they first lived in a warren of cells and chambers around Mary's room, looked after by the gentle, motherly woman who had, Vincent knew, lost children of her own. But around the age of eleven or twelve most children went looking for quarters of their own. On the whole the denizens of the world Below tended to live fairly close together, but there were many farther-flung chambers and rooms to choose from as well. Frequently the first apartments picked reflected a flare for the dramatic or ostentatious: a chamber called The Cathedral near the Catacombs was a favorite, until its inhabitants discovered—as they invariably did—how far it was from the warmth of the steam pipes, and how bad the only close-by source of water tasted.

Ho's room on the outskirts of the South Pockets, one of the farthest of those which could be considered in the perimeters of the inhabited sections at all, had been more or less inherited by her from a woman named Esther, one of the most ancient members of the community, who had been particularly fond of the scrappy, bitter little seven-year-old when she had first come among them. Esther had died when Ho was nine or ten, and many of her things had still been in the round, domed chamber in the South Pockets four years later when Ho had decided to take it over. To the clumsy Victorian chairs and the narrow bed carved, Vincent recalled, by Pascal's father, the girl had added her own collection of grubby books, of experimental paintings done under the tutelage of Elizabeth in the Painted Tunnels, of tools which hung on the rock walls among the Gods-Eyes and luck-charms the old priestess Narcissa had given Ho for helping her fetch water and mix herbs. In the place of honor on a shelf was a painting Esther herself had done, of her own father and brothers outside a synagogue in Lodz, strange, stiff forms in black with smiling eyes.

Two candles burned in wine bottles nearly covered with a variegated shell of drippings. There were blankets heaped on the battered sofa, as if someone else had been staying there—at a guess Laura, one of Ho's particular friends who frequently spent all or part of the night there talking, as teenagers will. A moment's search confirmed the guess—Vincent knew the property of

164

everyone in the Tunnels by sight, as, indeed, any member of that extended family could have identified the blue plaid poncho and that faded log-cabin quilt.

All this Vincent ascertained in a quick glance around the room. Then he ducked back out into the corridor again, taking one of the candles with him, stooping to look at the floor. It was raw rock here, and dry, showing him no track. Swiftly he padded along it to its end, where a short flight of steps led down to a long crossing-passage paved in discolored brick. He called out again, "Regan! Ho!" and listened while the echoes swallowed up his words.

There was no reply. If the flood was coming up the Brick Steps—and even from here, sniffing the air he could smell water from that direction—Ho and Laura, Regan and her children, would have been cut off from both sides. That meant they'd gone inward, into the mazes of tiny corridors and narrow chambers which few people fully knew, looking for another way out.

Vincent hurried his steps to the Brick Rooms to make sure. That curious succession of groined, brick-lined chambers, laid out like a railroad flat along a single line of ancient pipe, held nothing but Regan's few possessions and her children's toys. Taking a small metal souvenir of the Empire State Building in gold-painted copper from a shelf—he owned one like it himself and knew what a good tapping-key it made—Vincent went to the pipeline and rapped out a message to Pascal. *Any word Regan/Laura/Ho?* He waited. The South Pockets were deep, below the main tangled body of the master pipes, but still he could hear the muted reverberations of other messages chiming above and around him in the dark. Some of them he read, easily picking out Pascal's swift, abbreviated codes from among the more hesitant Morse and pseudo-Morse of less experienced senders.

Then, sharp and clear: *No word. Where?*

Brick rooms. Water up main shaft. Will search.

Blessings, came Pascal's reply. Vincent smiled; Pascal coded down whatever words he could, anything commonly used and understandable by all. It was typical of him that he'd have included a blessing in his limited vocabulary of single-tap.

And, thought Vincent grimly, picking up his candle again and turning back to the darkness, he was going to need it.

Thirteen

THEY wouldn't have gone down, thought Vincent, pausing in the chilly updraft of a natural shaft down which someone, in the distant past, had hung a ladder of rusted chain. *They'll be trying to go up.* He leaned out over the shaft, holding his candle aloft. Only darkness met his eyes—the shaft petered fifty or sixty feet up to something a child couldn't have crawled through, and at that point the iron crossbar from which the ladder dangled had been driven. The pit below was to all intents and purposes bottomless. As children Vincent and Devin had dropped countless lighted candles down it, trying to see how far down the lights would go, or old tin cans, listening for the final rattle. The wind blowing up the shaft had extinguished the falling candles; they had never heard the cans land.

Still, he called out "Ho! Regan!" raising his voice to the booming roar of which it was capable, and paused again to let the echoes die, listening. There was, if he recalled, a sort of passage leading nowhere out of the upper part of the shaft, and they might have conceivably gone that way, if any of them knew about it and thought it might get them anywhere.

And that was assuming, he added grimly to himself, that Regan and her children were with Ho and Laura—that he was looking for one party and not two. The water in the shaft of the Circular Stair, he guessed, was rising at the rate of six or seven inches a minute. It left him perhaps twenty minutes before the situation would become critical—before the distance underwater, down the shaft, into the main tunnel, out to the stair, became too long to be negotiated on a single lungful of air. At that point, he thought, moving down the narrow rock-seam toward another little-used tunnel he knew of which Ho or Regan might have construed as a possible exit, he would have to decide whether to abandon his quest for the little party, or to perish with them.

He hurried on, taking the turnings unthinkingly. The light of his feeble candle jerked and fluttered over the damp rock walls, his shadow, a black and monstrous lion-ghost, stalked behind. The tunnels of the South Pockets narrowed and grew more convoluted as they wound inwards, spiraling oddly up or downwards. Water crept down the walls here and seeped from the floor, and it was on the floor that Vincent finally saw a track.

It was a child's footmark, half-outlined as if Alec—Regan's six-year-old son—had trodden in one of the puddles. For a time there were no others, then, where clay instead of stone made up the uneven surface of the floor, he saw two more, a narrow foot in a soft boot that he knew to be Regan's, and the intricate circled pattern of a basketball sneaker that would be Ho's.

They were together, then. He breathed a sigh of relief.

The tunnel he had considered a likely possibility—one which looked as if it might lead somewhere, though it in fact did not—was blocked. Water trickled sluggishly from its dark mouth, mixed with filthy grayish silt—reaching down, Vincent touched it, and wiped his hand on the wet sleeve of his shirt.

Quicksand. The main must have ruptured into a near-by pocket, the leaking water flushing the stuff into the seam. Raising his candle, he looked down the dark corridor; he could see where it had broken through the wall, a thick vertical drift of it, blocking the passage in a wetly gleaming, porridgy mass.

Vincent crouched again, holding the candle close to the floor. If the fugitives had come this way the thin sheet of seep-water had obliterated any tracks. He walked carefully up to the mass, keeping an uneasy eye on the tunnel wall where, he knew, more of the deadly pocket would be pressing, and called out as loudly as he dared, "Ho! Regan!"

Listen as he would, and his ears were sharp, he could hear no reply.

Where else? He left the tunnel as swiftly as he could, for underground quicksands were among the greatest of the perils of the world Below: a break in the tunnel wall near a pocket could trap and smother a man in minutes. The South Pockets were appallingly well provided with little-explored tunnels and avenues that would look promising to those who had not actually investigated them. There was, he recalled, another upward-leading shaft near the Brick Steps. If Regan knew about that one they might have tried to escape that way.

Beside him, sharp and clear, he heard the clatter of his name on the pipes.

He stepped quickly over to the cluster of three that ran along the upper part of the wall at this point, rapped with the little Empire State model he still carried in his pocket to signal his presence.

Located. Located.

Where?

Lost. A long pause; he heard other pipes echo with the rapid-fire spatter of Pascal's taps, interrogating, and the dim, sympathetic vibration of a reply.

Then another long pause, and in his mind he saw Pascal and Mouse, sitting in the Pipe Chamber, conferring in quiet voices; saw, also, the water rising, black and inexorable, in the tunnel that led back to safety.

Another flurry of taps, the vibration more sensed now than heard. Pascal, he knew, would be listening to the pipe with his stethoscope, his bald head bowed, his eyes shut, his hands in their torn and battered gloves delicate as a surgeon's where they touched the thin cylinder of steel. The pipe-player loved his work with a passion shared by few men above the ground. He could talk for hours about the histories of the pipes, about what lines had been laid, and when, about the metals used in the manufacture and where the smallest conduits ran in the endless mazes of darkness. Sometimes in the dead hours of night, while Vincent prowled his eternal rounds in the Tunnels, he would go to the Pipe Chamber and pass the time with the gentle little man, listening to his tales of who had invented which codes, who had used them and why, why they had been changed; odd stories, some of them, like the way old Esther had communicated in Yiddish for years with some dweller underground whom no one else had ever seen, or how Pascal had stumbled into a way to communicate with a man in the Tombs who had lived in the Tunnels years before.

Rapid and sharp, the tapping came again. *Mouse says, downward spiral caves, second tunnel.*

It was the one blocked with quicksand. In his heart Vincent felt he'd known it all along.

He tapped back, *Sure? Little time.*

No time, he reflected to himself—this was going to be close, and error would drown them all.

A pause, while Mouse and Pascal conferred in the blazing gloom of that forest of candles among the crisscrossing universe of pipes. Then: *They don't know themselves, but tone of pipe tells me copper impurities in alloy typical of 'thirties, same as pipe Mouse says in that area. Sure.*

Vincent grinned to himself. Trust Pascal. He tapped back, *En route.*

Blessings.

The quicksand had seeped farther into the tunnel, spreading down it nearly to the entrance and all but blocking it completely. Grimly, Vincent waded into the filthy, softly moving stuff, digging with his powerful arms into the great wall of it that rose like a drift of putrid oatmeal before him. Fortunately it was firm enough to be pushed aside, but it would, he knew, flow back quickly. Moreover if the wall had weakened in one place there was no telling where else it would weaken once he was past this first inflow. Like a giant mole he tore and dug at the heavy clay, forcing his way past the blockage, and into the tunnel beyond.

As he'd feared, the floor there was ankle-deep in seep-water, telling him the walls had weakened elsewhere as well. He had extinguished the candle to dig. Removing it, and the carefully wrapped matches carried by all the dwellers Below, from his pocket he felt how little remained of the wax stub. In the guttering yellow match-light he noted uneasily how the ceiling was dripping, how the single line of pipe along the wall sagged where it had been bent out of shape by the pressures on the shifting rock, and he hurried forward, bare feet splashing in the ooze.

"Regan!" he called. "Ho!"

"Vincent!"

He ran.

They were huddled in a turning off the main tunnel: Ho and Laura, Regan and her two small children, and an old man named Anzac whom Vincent hadn't even known lived near the South Pockets, a withered old codger whose single remaining leg was augmented with a wooden stump and a crutch. The old man grinned when he saw Vincent and said, "Well, my Daddy told me of a giant ten-foot rat which lived in the sewers of London, and here you are, boy!"

Vincent glanced down at his shirt and breeches, dyed a uniform gray-green by quicksand and slime, and chuckled softly. His mane and the long hair on the backs of his hands were matted thick with the stuff; from his grime-plastered face his eyes caught the candlelight like amber mirrors. "Coming through the mazes I was beginning to feel like one. Quickly . . . the water's rising fast but there's a line out to the Circular Stair."

They were hurrying down the tunnel with him even as he and Anzac had traded their banter. Regan, a beautiful red-haired woman whose face bore the wear of tough years, carried her three-year-old daughter Jeanne in her arms; Laura, a sturdy dark-haired girl of fifteen, carried the six-year-old Alec. As they strode in Vincent's wake Ho translated Vincent's words in a swift flood of gestures to Laura, who was deaf, then turned toward Vincent and said, "We thought we could get out this way but it's blocked farther up, the ceiling's caved in, there's quicksand coming through."

"You wouldn't have gotten out in any case," said Vincent. "The tunnel turns downwards."

Her pointed little face was streaked with clay and grime, and, under the filth, her freckles stood out blackly against a pallor of exhaustion and dread. "Dammit, every tunnel we tried . . ."

"Told you the only ways out of this beehive were the Stair and the Brick Steps," retorted Anzac, stumping along beside the scrawny girl. His coat, cut down out of a tattered and indescribably ancient leather jacket, flapped as he limped along; his gloved hand moved smoothly, snakelike on the handle of his crutch.

"Yeah, but you also told me Australia was an independent nation and didn't have anything to do with the Queen."

"Well, if it ain't that way it ought to be, duckie."

"Duckie yourself."

"Show a little respect for an old man or I'll trip you with me stick."

The quicksand had oozed down to fill the tunnel once more, the wall of it widening, and Vincent attacked it with a kind of ferocious desperation, tearing and thrusting at the quivering stuff, half burrowing, half swimming through. It was wetter, runnier now, as the seeping floodwaters saturated it, and slid heavily down around him even as he dug. Behind him he heard the boy Alec whisper, "Is that quicksand, Mamma?" and Regan reply reassuringly, "Just mud, honey."

"Quickly," gasped Vincent, reaching back through the narrow wormhole he'd bored in the slowly moving drift. His arms were just long enough to catch the little boy's hands as Regan handed her son through to him; mud and water came slithering down from the main drift as Vincent pulled him through. He set the boy down behind him, then reached back, clawing and scraping as more mud oozed to fill the gap.

As he dragged Jeanne through he heard Alec say softly behind him, "Vincent . . ." and turning from his position halfway up the slippery mound, he could see what brought the note of fear to the child's voice. The tunnel behind them was sheeted over with a thin film of water.

Digging, scratching, hauling, he pulled the others through by main force, and, catching up Alec in his arms while Regan picked up her daughter once again, led the way back towards Ho's chamber at a run. The room was almost knee-deep when they reached it, muddy and sodden and beginning already to dissolve into ruin. Ho flinched back with a noise of sickened disgust, and turned her face away.

"Quickly," said Vincent, wading through the room to the door which led into the hall on the other side. "There's a cable tied to the top rung of the ladder; you should be able to pull hand-over-hand, out to the Circular Stair. It's a long pull." As he spoke, he was making a rapid estimate of relative strengths—his own, the children's, the women's. "Regan, take Jeanne. Tie her belt through yours. Ho, take Alec. I'll see to Anzac."

"The hell you will, sonny," snapped the old man. "I been hopping around on a crutch and a stick for nigh to forty years—I got arms like a tree. Those kids can't tail a rope fast enough to get 'em through."

Vincent opened his mouth to protest.

"And don't argue with me, it'll just waste your time and we got none to waste. You girls, git! Go!"

Ho and Laura traded a glance—Vincent gestured, confirming. He knew the old soldier was right. "Go. Follow the cable—it's a long way under-water, so go quickly. Wait. Give me your belts."

With his crutch Anzac began tapping out a message on the pipe: *All safe, all coming up.* Ho looked back at her room, flooded, slimy, ruined, everything she had made and treasured for herself in this life already coming to pieces. Beside her Laura watched her face, her own dark eyes filled with helpless compassion for her friend. Old Esther's painting of the Lodz ghetto bobbed briefly on the flood for a moment, then sank out of sight. Ho shrugged bitterly, and jerked her head at Laura. Together the two girls splashed empty-handed away into darkness.

Vincent dropped to one knee before the children, and gestured to their mother to follow the two girls.

"Alec, Jeannie," he said gently. "How long can you hold your breath underwater?" While he spoke he threaded Laura's heavy leather belt between the belts of the tiny girl and her brother, like the link of a chain, and Ho's between Alec's and his own. "A long time?"

"A hour," stated Alec confidently.

"Good." His clawed fingers flew, adjusting buckles, straps. "Jeannie?"

"Two hours," she affirmed, not fully understanding but not about to be outdone.

"Very good." The children were staring with fear-filled eyes as the filthy water streamed around them, the few juddering candles left in Ho's rooms seeming to increase rather than relieve the gloom. Around them the clanging of the pipes was much clearer, as rapid-fire messages outlined crises, problems, solutions: *flood in the Moss Cave, flood in the Dutch sewer; Randolph, Zach, and William trapped* . . .

Deliberately, he kept his voice calm. "Now take a deep breath," he instructed calmly. "Let it out . . . another . . . *big* breath . . . good." He heard old Anzac's retreating stride splash through the water in the shaft, then a muttered curse, and the sloshing whoosh of a dive.

"Time to go," he said. Lifting a child under each arm he hastened down the tunnel, water surging around his feet. He stepped into the blackness of what was rapidly becoming a well, treading water with the children bobbing beside him like corks. The water streaked their clay-covered faces with lines of white, dripped from their matted hair. Their eyes followed his movements nervously as he felt underwater for the guiding rope.

"Vincent."

He paused, shaking back his wet mane to look inquiringly at Alec, dog-paddling on the surface at his side.

"Do you think . . . Are there sharks in the water?"

"If there are," he said gravely, "they'll only hear you if you let your breath out, so we should all be

176

safe. Now, deep breaths . . . one . . . two . . . now!''

Small hands clutched at his belt as he plunged under. The children's small, awkward bulk impeded him, dragged him back with the force of the water as he pulled hand-over-hand at the cable. His strength was enormous but he had the sensation of moving through a river of cold treacle, thick and unyielding. The entrance of the tunnel below seemed twice as far down as it had been coming up, the tunnel itself eternal. He had nothing to think about now but dragging on the cable and holding his breath. His lungs were burning by the time he found the underwater corner. *What must it be to Alec and Jeanne?*

How long was sixty feet? How much farther to the Circular Stair? Had the others made it? What if the entry was blocked by debris, what if there was a rupture in the tunnel wall and quicksand was coming through somewhere? In any case the entry had to be completely underwater and who knew how far up the Stair . . .

His arms whipped through the water, hauling his own body and the two that bobbed behind it. His senses concentrated until the world was nothing but the rough smart of cable under his palms and the spear of pain in his chest. Then his head brushed stone. The cable was climbing. He turned in the water to drag himself out through the submerged door into the stair-shaft, struggled upward . . .

With a gasp of agony he broke surface, released the cable and grabbed a child with each hand, pulling them up on either side of him. Alec was coughing and retching; Jeanne only clung to his wrist, her breath sobbing. ''Mamma,'' she whispered, and Vincent caught her tight as her hands slacked and she passed out.

"Come on." One kick took Vincent to the pale stone curve of the stair. Lights bobbed distantly at the top; someone called out "There they are!" and he heard a cheer. Alec clung to his back, small hands gripping his mane, and with Jeanne's slight weight under one arm he heaved himself out of the surging black lake and stumbled up the stairs.

Regan, Ho, and Laura were at the top, wrapped in blankets and surrounded by a small knot of men and women in the pond of muddy kerosene light from a lantern set on the floor. Mary was with them, her dress wet to the knees and her hands bleeding from some unheeded abrasion gotten in rescue work, waiting to gather Regan's children into the quilts and afghans she so endlessly made. Behind her the tunnels were choked in darkness, save now and then for a jolting light where someone pelted on another rescue, another errand. Around them, the pipes kept their staccato drumfire . . .

> (Yet the ear distinctly tells
> In the jangling
> And the wrangling
> How the danger sinks and swells;
> By the sinking or the swelling in the anger
>   of the bells . . .
> In the clamor and the clanging of the bells!)

The moment Vincent emerged safe, Luke dropped his end of the rope and ran to Ho's side. Huddled under a blanket, her black braids soaked and straggling and her clothes sticking to her scarecrow frame, the girl pushed him impatiently away as he tried to put his arms around her protectively. He fell back, hurt and confused. Her arms wrapped around herself, Ho sat frozen, motionless as an angular little stone.

Regan and Mary were hugging one another and the children, both sobbing and stammering to one another with relief. Trailing an assortment of Mary's quilts, Laura came over to Vincent and gave him a wordless hug, then turned to go to Ho's side.

Vincent looked quickly around the darkness of the tunnel. "Anzac?"

At the sound of the old man's name Ho looked up at him, then away, bitterness tightening her mouth. Vincent met Laura's eyes.

Her face filled with grief, the deaf girl only shook her head.

"Told you so." Mouse turned to look around him at the assembled Tunnelfolk gathered in the Long Chamber, the flickering of a hundred lamps and candles augmented by the glow of two smoky fires built in open tin washtubs. "*Told* you."

The flood had spread through most of the lower section of the inhabited passageways, driving numerous individuals and groups from their chambers, cutting off others who had climbed into airshafts and isolated pockets above. In many of these areas the sole means of egress was up, through manholes and sub-basements into the world Above. Four or five little groups had taken this route, following Pascal's tapped instructions, hastening through the windswept, half-frozen alleys of the city overhead in the dead of night to other entrances, or to the homes of Helpers who passed them through the hidden doors, the secret cellars, and so Below again.

Other places, even very deep ones like the Chamber of Winds and Narcissa's secret domains, not connecting with the flooded sections, had been completely untouched.

One group near the Moss Cave was still cut off, from both above and below. They had food, and air, and could communicate through the pipes, but something would have to be done quickly about getting them out; Father and Winslow were already working on plans.

The old man Anzac had been the only casualty. A painstaking survey by Father showed everyone else accounted for, though many, like Ho, had lost all their possessions, some of them the last emotional links with their vanished lives Above. In the Long Chamber's corners a few little clumps of blankets and cooking utensils marked where two or three groups were camped while they looked for new quarters elsewhere in the Tunnels, or waited to see what would be done about the dark waters filling what had once been their homes.

Mouse turned to Father, who was seated on the Victorian ironwork arch of stairs that led up to the balcony which circled the Chamber's walls halfway up their thirty-foot height, and waved his arms expansively. "Okay good, okay fine—*now* get parts from Above?"

"The apprehensions you expressed about the state of the pump," replied the old man drily, "justify theft no more now than they did three months ago."

"Not *theft!*"

"No?" Ho, sitting with her arms locked around her knees at the foot of the steps, turned her head a little to look up at Father, her dark, Oriental eyes narrow and tired. They'd all been working salvage detail; nobody had had much rest.

"Father, we put out word to the Helpers three months ago, and what have we got? A couple hundred feet of PVC pipe, two manifolds that are the wrong size, a bucket of nuts and bolts and a flywheel Winslow's *still* tryin' to get into working order. It's not like we're proposin' to stick the place up at gunpoint, you know. Maybe we need to talk reality instead of theory here." Her face had aged, since the death of her old friend and the ruin of the only place she had slowly learned to call home.

"You want reality?" Winslow leaned his shoulder against the iron strut of the steps. He too looked exhausted in the grimy torchlight, for he'd been out working salvage, checking the length of the Old Main and any pipes which connected into it for more pressure-damage, repairing as best he could before the water could break through elsewhere. Vincent, patrolling the tunnels to their farthest extent, knew the job wasn't half done yet.

"I'll tell you about reality. Reality is that if they start huntin' for thieves, with half the tunnels cut off from the other half, we got noplace to run."

Ho got to her feet and waved furiously, helplessly. "The fact that half the tunnels are cut off from the other half is the reason we need a pump! A couple of pumps, now!"

"And generator," added Mouse. "Can build generator easy, just need—"

"Not *now*, Mouse!" Ho's hand sliced the air, a gesture for silence like an unspoken curse. Then she turned back to Father, sitting on the steps with Vincent standing on the level of the floor by his side. "Don't you see?" She swung around, surveying the assembled men, women and children who sat or stood close about them in the low aureate shadows of the candles, the great vaulted chamber echoing with the soft thunder of the subway lines above. "That stuff should be our first priority."

"No," said Father quietly. "Our first priority is to have a world unlike the one from which we take sanctuary here. I'm sorry, I truly am. But the alternative you suggest is not an option for us. Mary, if word can be got out to the Helpers about this . . ."

With a strangled noise of frustration the girl whirled, her dark gaze passing from face to face, challenging Winslow, Jamie, Laura, seeking for some show of support. In despair she turned at last toward Luke, standing mute and helpless at the front of the crowd. Vincent saw their gaze hold for a moment. Then Luke's eyes dropped.

Father had turned to listen to Mary as she spoke of other ways of obtaining the parts to fix the pumps, to Winslow's plan for cannibalizing some of the other pumps in the Tunnels to work at clearing out at least some of the water on the lower levels. But Vincent, like Ho, acutely aware of the limitations of this sanctuary world, followed the girl with his eyes as, with bowed head, she pushed her way in silence through the crowd in the shadowy Chamber, leaving the feeble puddles of lamp flame and candlelight for the chilly dark of the Tunnels beyond. Luke took a few steps after her, reaching out helplessly, but she was beyond him. He stopped with her name unspoken, only able to watch her stride away.

Fourteen

V INCENT?''

Echoes traded his name back and forth down the shadowy crossing of galleries and mains. Down here near the Great Waterfall and the Abyss, the flood had not penetrated, though these areas were far deeper than the course of the Old Main—the noise of the subways was left far behind, and even the tapping of the pipes came only distantly through the utter dark. Vincent paused, listening. The echoes made it difficult to tell, for the whisperer was a great distance away, probably back near where the Iron Stair went down to the Chamber of the Winds. But he thought it was a girl.

For a moment he heard only the drip of water, the whisper of underground winds. Then the soft, flickering echo of steps.

Because he was scouting for damage and intrusion—there was no telling how far water had seeped from the flooded areas, or where it might be building up in quicksand pockets again—Vincent carried candles and a small lantern, but he carried them unlit. Even in this pitchy blackness his night-sighted eyes could distinguish the anomalies that might spell danger, and he guided himself in the Tunnels' dark as much by touch, scent, and hearing as by sight. In any case he was far less dependent upon sight alone than those with human senses, and any light made him less able, for several minutes, to see accurately in the darkness after.

He moved back up the tunnels with the soft-footed silence of a huge cat, scanning the dark walls for any flicker of reflected light. The searcher would be carrying some. At the top of a long brick ladder-well he stopped, and called out, "Stay where you are!"

. . . *you are . . . you are . . . are . . . are . . . are* . . . The echoes picked up his call like a relay of ghosts.

"Vincent?" It was more definite, closer—Jamie's voice.

"I'll come to you. Speak."

A long pause. Then, *"Now is the winter of our discontent made glorious by this sun of York."*

Vincent, padding noiselessly after the echoes, smiled inwardly. The small and secluded community of the Tunnelfolk valued books and poetry, and between reading and the amateur theatricals at Winterfest almost everyone could recite long passages by heart. But Father, he thought, would be disappointed at this mundane usage of his hero's greatest works.

All the children did it, when lost in the galleries.

"Now are our brows bound with victorious wreaths; our bruised arms hung up for monuments, our stern alarms changed to merry meetings."

The echoes grew less confusing, their time shortening up as he neared the speaker. Ahead he saw the sulfurous glimmer of kerosene light against the damp rock wall.

"Now instead of . . . of . . . of mounting barbed steeds to fright the souls of fearful adversaries, he capers nimbly in a lady's chamber to the lascivious playing of a lute."

Wryly, as he made his way toward the light and toward Jamie's increasingly uncertain voice, Vincent finished the soliloquy in his mind. She hadn't remembered how it ended, of course. Most of the kids never got past the first dozen lines.

I, that am curtailed of this fair proportion, cheated of feature by dissembling nature, deformed, unfinished, sent into this breathing world scarce half made up . . . have no delight to pass away the time, unless to spy my shadow in the sun and descant on mine own deformity.

Coming around a corner he found her, lantern in hand, in the junction of a long, brick-roofed seam where water leaked sluggishly down the walls. She'd dried on Richard III's opening monologue and was looking around her at the close-pressing shadows, a tall, slim girl of sixteen or seventeen, fair and blue-eyed and pretty, dressed in the usual conglomeration of quilted vest and leather-patched breeches, her soft boots splashed with mud and slime. From the darkness he gravely quoted a line from Hamlet, *"Stand and unfold yourself,"* and she turned around with a breathy laugh at the aptness of it, but her thin oval face grew grave again at once as she hurried toward him.

"Oh, Vincent, I'm so glad I found you!"

"What's happened?"

Her mouth twisted, wry with exasperation and concern. "It's Mouse. He's gone to the surface to get parts to repair the pump."

There were times, thought Vincent, when he could have taken his friend and shaken him till his teeth rattled. Not that such an activity would do any good.

"I thought he needed men to help."

"He's got Ho with him."

Vincent bowed his head, stabbed, not with surprise, but with resigned and profound regret. When he read the *Iliad* he always hoped that this time Achilles would say, *Patroklos, I couldn't POSSIBLY let you wear my armor into battle, but if you feel that strongly about it, I'll lead the troops myself.* So far Achilles never had. Perhaps Ho's defection was equally inevitable.

So he only asked, "Do you know the way?"

The Nassau Street Local ceased operation at eight P.M., so Vincent and Jamie had to make their way to the 14th Street–Canarsie line, which ran all night. Several blocks away from the First Avenue Station they doused the lanterns and left them hidden, and at Vincent's whispered instructions, Jamie climbed a narrow shaft which would debouch, he knew, into the steam tunnels beneath the Beth Israel Medical Center. From there she could exit into an alley behind 17th Street. Though no one in the Tunnels used money the children habitually collected subway tokens, trading them for favors or trinkets amongst themselves, and all of them, moreover, were past masters at the cadging of free rides.

Vincent himself took a repair-duct to an access-hatch just beyond the station in the subway tunnel itself, waiting as close to the grainy electric glow that penetrated from the station as he dared. Through the round arch of yellow light he could hear and smell the packed humanity of the place. It was eleven o'clock at night, and the platform was full, the smell of cigarettes, the stink of vagrants' clothing and whores' perfume, the unending yammer of voices and the dinning of traffic up top, all swirling around him like a dirty river as he waited for the deep thunder of the train.

In spite of Father's lectures he knew that the kids he'd grown up with in the Tunnels—Mitch, Devin, Scott, and the others—had all had a try at riding the subways at some time or another. He himself had always been good at it, with his effortless strength and animal timing, though as a child he'd seen one boy killed. It was a very fast death.

The darkness around him shuddered with the approach of the train. Looking from behind the concrete abutment which concealed him, Vincent could see, at the opposite end of the long station, the scorching white eye of the train's headlamp as it entered the station.

It stopped with a virulent hissing of steam brakes. The smell of hot metal and oil burned in Vincent's nostrils, and the stench of humanity suddenly increased as the crowd pressed forward into the open doors, struggling momentarily with the outbound wave. He hoped Jamie would have the rudeness and strength to make it onto the car. If not, they would be delayed—perhaps fatally, for Mouse and Ho. But under no circumstances would he countenance Jamie taking the fast way and riding the top of the car with him.

The brakes hissed again, and Vincent braced himself. The cars accelerated wickedly fast.

The second the headlamp was past him he darted from cover, cleared the narrow catwalk by the track in a stride. The train was just starting to pick up speed as he made his leap, catching the edge of the roof in powerful claws and flipping himself up like a cat leaping onto a windowsill, then lying flat, arms spread and claws dug into the worn and splintery slats. Overhead the darkness crackled with the ozonic smell of electricity; wind raked his hair and his mantle, and the dark thunder of the train's speed shook his bones.

Father had always been horrified about it, but Vincent thoroughly enjoyed riding the cars.

When the train began to decelerate for the Bedford Street Station Vincent dropped off, knees taking his weight springily on the catwalk well beyond the glow of the station's lights. He dropped immediately back into cover and made his way to the nearest repair-duct, and so down into the steam tunnels again. There he waited, near the manhole entrance on Berry Street he'd instructed Jamie to find.

She appeared a few minutes later, hands shoved deep in her jeans pockets and boots slapping in the scummy water which had collected in the tunnel after the last rain. "Some jerk tried to pick me up in the station," she informed him when she got near. "It beats me why people live up there at all."

They followed a steam tunnel that paralleled Berry Street, went down a broken twist of forgotten stone steps to an older seam passing under sub-basements and water-mains. They were close to the river, and the moisture collecting on the walls and puddled on the floor had a sewery stink. There were no lights here, but Jamie, like all members of the Tunnel community, carried a candle and matches, and by the dim gold light Vincent could easily pick out Ho's and Mouse's tracks in the slime.

In the basement of what had been a warehouse on Kent Avenue they emerged from belowground, the grubby radiance of the city around them filtering through ceiling-beams still charred from a fire which had gutted the place ten years ago, bright to Vincent's eyes. At this hour the neighborhood by the old docks was nearly deserted, even the homeless seeking other places to sleep, out of the cutting January cold. Their breath a faint trail of steam, Vincent and Jamie slipped unseen across the filthy concrete floor, still littered with blackened debris, puddled water, and the trash that accumulates in any deserted building from vermin and transients, and out a broken door into an alleyway hemmed in by corrugated fences. Vincent had brought up his hood to cover his head, deeply uneasy as he always was above the ground, listening, watching, smelling the air. Somewhere a boat's horn hooted. An alley cat slipped by, a ghost among the ash-cans. Loading cranes, like bizarre mechanical birds, loomed against the sky. Closer to, a couple of disused piers, creaking with rust and dry rot, huddled like a junked barricade in front of the fire-hemmed black mirror of the river.

And beyond that barricade, beyond the river, New York soared in a triumphant wall of light.

Her world, thought Vincent, pierced to the heart by the sight of it as he stood outside it, distant, in this ruin of tumbledown buildings and smelly puddles, broken masonry and scrap metal, the bitter night wind stirring at the ends of his hair.

That was what she was. A woman who dwelled in those towers of light. But the thought, which he had expected to turn him away from her, to press home to him the impossibility of his dreams, only made him remember her kindness to him, the occasional flash of her wry humor even in the depths of her pain and unhappiness, the touch of her hand on his. He had nothing to offer her, nothing to give. In that Father was absolutely right. But where he stood in the grime of the alley, if she had appeared suddenly on the opposite shore of the East River and held out her hand to him, he knew he would have been in the water and swimming.

With an effort he turned away.

"Here," Jamie breathed.

The sign over the gate said, STAN'S STUFF—BUY ANYTHING, RENT ANYTHING, SELL ANYTHING. Behind a cyclone fence a pre-fab guardhouse stood in a yard filled with an elephant's graveyard of machinery—backhoes, forklifts, electric trucks, concrete-cutters, a bulldozer like a sleeping triceratops and endless numbers of old oil drums and tires. A couple of floodlights mounted on twelve-foot four-by-fours threw a dirty yellow illumination over everything, giving the warehouse that stood in the middle of the yard and the rust-grimed, tumbledown remains of an old pier behind it a cut-edged look of significance they never would have had by day. Behind them New York's lights made a glowing background, like a jeweled velvet scarf upon which a rusted-out carburetor had been carelessly set.

Vincent glided along the perimeter until he found the place where the barbed wire that topped the fence had been neatly snipped by Mouse's bolt cutters. "Wait for me here," he breathed to Jamie. "Whistle if you see anyone. If anyone sees you, get out of sight. If—"

From the direction of the warehouse a flashlight beam darted, making them both duck. A man yelled, "Freeze, you little— Damn!" There was a crash of falling metal, a scurry of flying feet.

"Danny?" yelled another voice, and Vincent heard a heavy man's thudding tread among the grease-streaked heaps of metal that blocked his view.

"See anything?"

"There!"

The scamper of flight again, and the crack of a gun, the bullet panging noisily on something steel. Vincent and Jamie shrank back around the corner of the alley, Vincent listening hard, gauging by the wheezing breath of the heavier guard, the creak of a straining pants-belt and the occasional scrape and clang of metal the course of the pursuit. The other guard swore again, and a second shot cracked out. A moment later Vincent heard the metallic groan and rumble of the warehouse door shutting, then the slam of a bolt.

"Martin! I got one of 'em!"

The thudding pursuit had stopped. A moment later Vincent heard Martin's panting voice saying, "Got away."

"Other one's locked in the warehouse. You phone the cops. The bastard might be armed—let's let them handle this."

"Amen to that, pal. You got a padlock? Little sleaze had bolt cutters. Thanks. The other one might come back."

"You want to bet on that? Little nigger probably ain't stopped runnin' yet."

Behind him Vincent heard the light ringing of the wire fence. Rising soundlessly to his feet he saw Ho wriggling under a bent-up place in the wire. He was standing over her before she got to her feet.

"Vincent!" For the first second all that was on her face was exhausted gratitude to see him—she would have thrown herself into his arms like a tired child if she hadn't remembered where she was. She stopped herself, and look down, dusky skin flushing with embarrassment.

Vincent reached out and gathered her into a quick hug of reassurance. At this point being angry at her would help nothing. The thin arms squeezed his rib cage gratefully. Then she backed off, shame-faced and scared.

A lot of things didn't need to be said. She knew them all; he could see it in her face and the slump of the narrow shoulders. So he said only, "Is there another way out of the warehouse?"

She shook her head. "Mouse checked."

That ended that possibility. If Mouse couldn't find egress, it was not there to be found. "Can you cut the electricity to the yard lights? We have to do this quickly, before the police arrive." Through the window of the pre-fab shack he could already see Martin, the fat guard, red-faced and sloppy in a wrinkled uniform, talking on the phone.

Ho nodded. She was shivering, her breath a scrim of steam in the dingy glare. Her freckles stood out sharply across dust-colored skin from which all excess color seemed to have been drained. But she pulled a pair of rudely insulated wire cutters from her jerkin pocket, and without a word slid back under the fence.

Vincent padded swiftly back to where Jamie waited under the cut place in the barbed wire, and shed his bulky coat. His voice was barely a whisper. "Wait here for me. In case of trouble get back to the burned warehouse."

It was all he had time for. Without warning the lamps on their tall poles blinked out; the dim bluish square of the guard-shack's window, too. One leap took Vincent to the top of the fence; he dropped to the ground and was sprinting between the rusted-out tractors and humped, dark donkey-engines before Jamie could draw breath to reply.

There was yelling from the guard-shack, indistinct and profane. The bolt on the warehouse door was heavy and padlocked. Vincent's clawed hand dug into the wood, gripping and tearing, and with a splintering shear it came free. At the same moment he heard the grating zigzag of sirens, and red and blue lights fluttered over the black cutouts of machinery. The police were arriving in force. He threw his shoulder to the door and slid it back. "Mouse!" he yelled to the oil-rank darkness inside.

Ringing footsteps sounded within. From behind him voices yelling, expostulating, swearing. A bullet whanged loudly off the cement near his head, a voice yelled, "You see anything?" and Mouse emerged, panting and white and badly scared.

White spotlight swept the wall. Vincent and Mouse ducked it and fled toward the shelter of the nearest forklift, Vincent feeling horribly naked without his concealing hood. He feared few things—it was not his nature to worry about physical threats and would not have been even had he not been powerful enough to cope with most of them—but the thought of capture turned him cold. Even being seen by outsiders bothered him deeply. Not only did he dread the horrors of incarceration for its own sake, but he knew that his very existence was the weak point in the safety of the Tunnels: the questions of his origin, of where he had lived to grow to maturity, of who had fed and clothed him, would inevitably suggest themselves to anyone who cornered him, and at that point,

Father's hard-won, hard-protected sanctuary would be over.

Blue-clothed men were everywhere along the fence. "I see them!" someone yelled, from over where they couldn't possibly be glimpsed, and someone else shouted, "Freeze!" Another shot plowed the oil-soaked ground and Mouse and Vincent fled around the corner of the warehouse building, Vincent's quick ears picking up the footsteps of pursuit.

Here was black and smelly chaos, where everything that couldn't be disassembled or reassembled for sale or re-use was haphazardly heaped; stripped chassis, dented quarter-panels, engine blocks with the guts ripped from them. Oily rags and yellowed newspapers littered the ground between the black, labyrinthine piles; the sewer smell of the river, the stink of ancient rags, of rotting fish, of human waste and long-dead animals, filled the air like a greasy slime. Vincent and Mouse broke apart, threading their separate ways among the gutted wasteland toward the creaking skeleton of the pier.

The lights pursued them.

Vincent dodged a searchlight and went to ground, crouching behind the crushed ruins of a '63 Impala half-filled with old newspapers and oil cans to watch a uniformed cop run past, two feet of black metal flashlight gripped like a club in his hand. The night was fiercely cold, the wind off the river sharp after the stillness of Below, cutting like a honed razor through the worn linen of Vincent's shirt sleeves and thick leather and quilting of this vest. Silently, Vincent backed, and slipped around a small Everest of eviscerated refrigerators and washing machines, moving away from the voices and the lights.

The police—six or eight of them, by the sound—had formed a cordon and were moving through the yard, flashlights swinging, guns in hand. Vincent thought he heard the jangling of the chain-link fence down near the foot of the pier and hoped that was Mouse and not some poor vagrant with the life half-scared out of him by the chaos. Cautiously he moved back again, heading for the pier. In its shadows he could take to the river, swim silently downstream and emerge elsewhere, to make his way back to the nearest way down before dawn.

But they seemed to have thought of that one. A man was already poking around in the darkness under the slime-footed pilings, flashlight beam winking off the fetid scum where the ground met the river. Vincent crouched in the shadows, hearing the random grind of utility shoes on gravel behind him, the crossing of voices. He'd have to wait till the man turned, and move fast . . .

Movement in the darkness beyond the fence caught his eye, and he realized it was Mouse a split second before the rock tossed by the little man hit the water behind the cop's back. The cop, burly and white-haired, swung around, flashlight striking a thousand yellow splatters from the water, and in the same eye blink Vincent was moving, leaping up the fence and onto the pilings of the pier.

To his horror the pilings yielded sickeningly under his weight, the whole pier swaying above him. It was rotted to its marrow bones and ready to collapse. Flashlight beams slashed and crossed in the darkness, catching his white shirt sleeves, the blond flag of his mane.

He edged out further, seeking darkness. The tie braces creaked and rocked drunkenly around him like an aspen grove in a gale. Light struck the pilings, making tangled shadows in the moving struts.

A voice from the shore boomed, "We can see you up there! Come down or we'll shoot!" A span cracked and gave beneath him; he pulled his foot quickly back, slipped around a post and tried again. He couldn't let himself be cornered. Even to be seen was unthinkable.

He was well over water now, but among the pilings he stood too good a chance of striking something with a jump and knocking himself out, or, worse, hanging himself up on the maze of braces below him. He gauged the distance toward the edge, trying in the crazy-house shadows to determine if the struts would take his weight. There was a greater chance that the officers' lights would strike him there, but at least he'd be in the clear to drop. The shift of his weight made the whole structure curtsy, the beams heaving and leaning around him so that he clung to the brace where he stood, waiting for stillness again.

"Riggs, Byrne," said a voice on the shore. "Go out and see what you can do."

Two blue-clothed forms strode forward in the darkness, scrambling up the piles, and Vincent knew he had to jump. As he moved toward the clear edge ahead of him the nearer of the two cops lost his grip, falling against a post, and the weight heaved the whole pier in a long sideways ripple. There was the crack of splintering wood; a man's voice swearing. Vincent gripped the reeling post beside him, trying to gauge his time, and at that moment the second cop lost his balance and fell.

With a horrible rending noise the pier heeled over, splitting in the middle in a rain of rotted logs, metal braces, splintered planks. Vincent dropped and hit water that stank like a cesspool, striking out desperately to get clear. Something crashed into his back with the weight and velocity of a falling tree. He gasped as his head went under, his whole body numb, fighting for air, for strength in his arms to get him out of this.

Catherine, he thought, *Catherine on the far shore, holding out her hands* . . .

He broke the surface, water streaming from his mane and eyes, tried to swim. He was hung up on something, being dragged down again; *I will die*, he thought, *and she will never know*. They'd tell Father, of course, but not her.

And he'd have missed it. Missed whatever it was with her, whatever it was to be. Missed it all.

He kicked clear of the underwater obstruction, swam upwards desperately. Just as his head emerged and he gasped in air, the rest of the pier, hanging in a suspended ruin against the livid sky, let go. His last sight was of the blazing skyline of New York, the city of ten thousand lights, as the torrent of plank and metal and snapping cables poured down over his head, and he sank like a stone.

Fifteen

CATHERINE needed him.

In his dreams Vincent prowled the Tunnels, hurrying back toward his room off the Long Chamber, soft boots silent on the stone floors, dark mantle billowing like storm cloud in his wake, hastening through the shadow-world Below toward where she lay. She had been hurt, broken in her faith and her courage; she needed his help, his love. He could see her lying in the soft tangle of dark furs and the quilts Mary had sewn or crocheted, weeping as he had found her weeping after she'd thrown the reflector at him, after she'd seen him for the first time. He reached out his hand to comfort her . . .

If I profane by my unworthiest hand . . .

But she wasn't there. He was walking again, this time Above. It was early night, and the bright-lit streets about him were crowded with the people of the day. Vincent in his dream strode through them unheeding, listening for her voice, knowing where she lived—that white building across from the park, those latticed terrace doors through which shined soft apricot light—hurrying there, hurrying as swiftly as he could, lest he be too late. Men and women in beautiful clothing shrank back from him; a dog being walked by a uniformed bellman barked wildly; cars jerked screeching to a stop by the curb. But none of it troubled him. He had to find her, find her soon and tell her . . .

Tell her what?

She was calling his name.

He knew it.

He knew it, even when the voice changed to Jamie's, and the dream dissolved into the foul taste of slimy water in his mouth and the bone-hurting cold of deep night above the ground. A ship's whistle groaned. Somewhere a police car went by, sirens braying, in pursuit of some other fugitive in the night.

"Vincent!" pleaded Jamie's voice.

"Vincent . . ." whispered Mouse, and a hand shook his shoulder. "Vincent, not die. Please-please-please not die."

"If I do not," said Vincent, trying to raise himself on one elbow and subsiding at once as every wrenched muscle of his back flinched in protest, "it will not be for want of assistance in that direction by my friends." He opened his eyes and looked out through the matted and filthy tangles of his mane to see Ho, Mouse, and Jamie kneeling around him in the deep gloom of the burned warehouse's subcellar.

With an inarticulate noise of joy Mouse threw his arms around him, heedless of the bruises that covered Vincent's shoulders and back. Vincent returned the embrace wholeheartedly in spite of the pain, glad only to see them all safe. Then, rather gingerly, he struggled to a sitting position. His mantle lay over him like a blanket. Without it he would certainly have frozen, for the January night was icy, the breath of the three teenagers a pallid haze in the diffuse light from the broken hatchway above. All three of them were soaked and shivering, the girls' long hair hanging in strings over their eyes. They must have gone into the river after him—even Mouse, who could barely swim—and pulled him from under the floating debris.

He pulled his mantle over his shoulders, drew the two girls under it for warmth. "Come," he said softly. "It's time we started back."

"You all right to travel?" Ho looked worriedly up at him. "You got banged up pretty bad."

An understatement, thought Vincent, pushing the strands of his mane out of his eyes. He could feel half-dried blood sticking to his shirt, matting the short fur of his shoulders and back. "Have I a choice?"

She looked away unhappily. Mouse, Vincent knew, had acted in his usual blithe, amoral innocence, but Ho knew that she had done wrong. All the way back, through the deep, claustrophobic seams far beneath the river—for Vincent knew that none of them were in any shape to jump onto a moving subway car—none spoke, and when Vincent returned to his chamber he fell into bed and slept like the dead.

He woke, and lay thinking about Catherine.

This was nothing new. He had thought of her, in the quiet lassitude which follows dreams, since they had parted, more than half a year ago. But he thought of drowning in the black waters of the river beneath that jeweled wall of lights; thought of dying without ever seeing her again.

Had we but world enough, and time, the poet

Marvell had written, to a lady who would not accept him into her arms and bed.

World enough, and time. Not to seduce, thought Vincent, but to let himself be seduced by the part of him that said, *I want what can be.* He was no less cognizant of the desperation of his position, no less conscious of Father's concerns for his safety, and for the safety of the whole delicate world Below.

But no one had sufficient world, or time. And there was something out there that he could have died last night without ever having touched.

> *But at my back I always hear*
> *Time's winged chariot hurrying near,*
> *And yonder all before us lie*
> *Deserts of vast eternity . . .*

"Vincent?"

He had heard Ho's light, firm step on the stair from the Chamber outside. As he turned his head and said, "Come," he winced at the stab of pain in the stiffened muscles of his back. When he sat up, however, bad as the ache in his body was, his head no longer hurt, and his vision was clear. *No concussion, then.*

Ho came quietly down the steps into his room. She stood beside his bed and looked at him for a moment, a skinny, plain girl with a sharp little face and Oriental eyes, and he saw again the ragged street child Jamie had brought down with her from Above one night, scared and dirty and fierce.

She fetched in her breath, and let it out with a sigh. "Thank you," she said simply. "Thank you for saving us. I've told Father."

Vincent pushed back his hair, rufous gold against

the tattered linen of his shirt. "You didn't have to."

"I was afraid you might have a concussion. He'd have to know how you'd been hurt. And besides," she added, "I didn't . . . I wanted him to know. I said I'd gone alone. Mouse can tell him about his part in it or not, whatever he wants. But I didn't want to lie."

Vincent nodded. When Father was angry his incisive logic could raise blisters on those who had gone against the community's rules. It took a good deal of courage to let oneself in for that.

"And I've been thinking," she went on after a moment. "I figured out where we can get the parts. Without stealing them, I mean. Just 'taking,' like Mouse says." She smiled a little, with bittersweet amusement at her friend's ingenuousness. "There must be a thousand scrap yards around Brooklyn and Jersey City, full of old stripped cars and dead washing machines, just left to rot. It'll take awhile, but we can go in and salvage parts. I could pull an engine when I was eight—my stepbrother used to strip cars on the streets clean in sixty seconds. But even the things they throw out in junkyards have lots of machine in them yet."

"If you say so," said Vincent, whose upbringing made it hard for him to picture a society so wasteful as to throw away anything that could conceivably be re-used, recycled, refitted. "Did you speak to Father of this?"

"Yeah." She nodded, and took another deep breath. "I said I'd be in charge of it, of getting the parts. I know what to look for. Probably without Mouse along, though, since I don't want to have that Stealing vs. Taking argument with him again

in some scrap yard up top. He just doesn't understand." She shrugged wryly. "And when that's
done . . . I'm leaving the Tunnels, Vincent."

He was silent, his clawed hands folded, looking
up into her eyes.

"I can't . . . I can't go on like this," she said,
desperation in her voice. "This world . . . it's good,
it's safe, it's gentle, but I need what it can't give
me." The sweep of her thin arm took in the
candlelit room with its carved doorway and Tiffany
lamp, the gallery outside where the last few
flooded-out groups still camped around their
smudge-pot fires, the whole secret complex of
catacomb and steam pipe, main and seam, stair and
tunnel and the dark abysses of the night.

"Vincent, I don't want to live my life having to
scrounge for food and clothing, having to raid
junkyards to get enough scrap to help out my
friends. I don't want to . . . to see people I care
about die because of some stupid disaster that
could have been avoided by having the right thing
at the right time." She shook her head, and her
voice cracked for a moment with bitterness. Vincent
remembered his friend Devin, saying much the
same thing—Devin's mother had died in childbirth,
and though he'd never known her, Devin had
always halfway blamed the simplicity of the life in
the Tunnels for that.

Taking a deep breath, she went on, "And I don't
want to end up marrying Luke or Scott or one of
the other guys here just because they're the only
guys I know, the only guys I've ever met. I feel
there's things out there I need to learn, need to
know, that nobody down here can teach me. I can
do somethin' up there now, I know I can—only I
don't know what! But I want to find out."

"What will you do?" he asked softly, remembering those others he had grown up with—Devin, and the dark-browed, angry Mitch—who, like Ho, had dreamed their widely separate dreams of the lands of light beyond the darkness.

Loving his world and the people in it as he did, he was not sure whether having a choice, as those others did, or not having one, was more painful.

Ho rubbed her hands, gloved as usual against the Tunnels' chill. "At first, board with one of the Helpers, and take night classes, and do temp work or flip burgers or do whatever I have to, to pay my way. I've got to know what's out there, Vincent. When I came down here I was a kid. I didn't know anything beyond the streets. I was little, I was hurting, and I needed a place to . . . to heal. And the Tunnels gave me that. But now I've seen—I've seen all the bits and pieces of it, Father's books, and Elizabeth's art, and Mary's nursing, and Winslow's and Mouse's little tinker-machines . . . and I've got to learn more. I've got to know where I can fit in."

She stepped forward and took his hands, looking down at him, those dark eyes without their wariness for once, pleading with him to understand. "You know, I looked out across that river last night, and I saw the world, those great big buildings filled with light like they were on fire. And I thought, 'I've got to have that. Whatever it is, it's out there. It's not Below.' Maybe there's somebody out there, somebody I need to meet. Do you understand?"

"Yes," said Vincent softly. "I understand."

"I can't live halfway, Vincent. I can't smell it, and taste it, and not hold it in my hands."

"No," he agreed.

*(. . . and tear our pleasures, with rough strife,
through the iron gates of life . . .)*

Tears stood in those black-coffee eyes that he'd
never seen so much as misty. She leaned forward
swiftly and hugged him, hard skinny wristbones
biting into his shoulders through the quilting and
leather of his vest. Then she straightened up and
was gone.

Vincent sat listening to her footsteps retreat
across the vestibule and down the stairs, and, it
seemed, down the Long Chamber, long after he
knew she was out of actual earshot. The pipes
clanked softly, Pascal relaying his eternal messages
from one part of the Tunnels to another; a subway
rushed softly by overhead.

"You didn't hear anything I said tonight."

Tom, pausing in the act of reaching to open the
door of her building for her, regarded Catherine
with eyebrows arched in surprise. If she hadn't
seen his "Who, me?" expression a thousand times
before—if she hadn't seen it done better by fifteen-
year-old street punks confronted with evidence of
activities ranging from lying to the police to drive-
by murder—she would have accepted that
surprised, slightly hurt expression for what it was
intended to convey: "I didn't know I was doing
anything wrong, how can you blame me for that?"

"What?" he said. "That your work's important
to you? I can understand that. My work's important to me. That doesn't mean we can't see each
other."

And, leaning forward, he kissed her on the lips.
She turned her face slightly aside, and kept her lips

closed, and after one try for more he drew back, regarding her with that same look she remembered so clearly from that night eight months ago at the Barron: a display of wounded concern thinly overlying annoyance.

In theory, she supposed, Tom's refusal to take no for an answer was the reason he was who he was: a wealthy young real estate developer with a skyrocketing career instead of the owner of a cheap schnitzel-joint in Calumet City like his father. In practice it meant that telling him anything he did not want to hear was a maddening exercise in evasion and pursuit.

But over the past several months she'd gotten a lot of practice in holding conversations with people who didn't want to talk.

Their date that evening had been the kind of outing she'd have been delighted with a year ago. They'd gone to see Michael Dorsey in *The Iceman Cometh*, and had dinner at Alcazar, a high-class Spanish restaurant in the upscale section of the Village. These days, after weeks of hastily snatched burgers and rubbery egg specials at Tummy Time, she valued the leisured elegance of good restaurants, which she had formerly taken for granted. Tom had been on his best behavior, as he had all through the holidays: for Christmas he had given her a delicate gold chain, and an ounce of Eternity perfume. It was only because Catherine had been determined to speak to him over supper about their relationship, uncomfortably balanced on "hold" for so long, that she had noticed how deftly he steered clear of anything resembling a personal or serious subject.

She sighed. He had been good to her in many

ways, and she did not want to hurt him. "Tom, things change."

He shook his head, half smiling but with that air that never failed to irritate her these days, the older-and-wiser expression, the you'll-thank-me-later-darling look. "I think you're carrying this new seriousness a little far." He took her shoulders lightly between his hands, the loving firmness in his voice masking what she now realized was a grim determination not to let go of something he wanted. "Listen, we're not going to be just friends. That won't work. It's not enough."

Her eyes met his. "It'll have to be," she said.

His brow creased a little in a frown, as if he did not understand. "Cathy," he said, like a father to a headstrong child, "knock it off. Look, you're working too hard. Let's go away this weekend, let's get some sun. Antigua . . . Jamaica . . ."

It had been on that weekend in the Bahamas they had first become lovers, on a beach beneath a luminous full moon. More rain was predicted for tomorrow, and the wind was freezing where it came whipping around the corner of the building. A year ago she would have jumped at the chance to get the hell out of New York in the middle of January. Impulse trips had always delighted her—the pleasant disorientation of shopping in the hot Jamaica sunlight when she'd breakfasted listening to the patter of New York rain. Her father, she remembered, had gotten her into that habit. How many places had she run to for a little mindless fun, when things got rough in college?

All Tom's little ploys—first the kidding, then the guilt, then the bribe, then the firm father . . . Had they always been that obvious?

She stepped back gently out of his grip. " 'Night, Tom."

His hands caught hers. "I'm not going to let you slip away," he said softly. "I won't let that happen."

He drew her to him again and kissed her, harder, demanding. Curious, she thought, how someone she had been that familiar with, someone she had slept with, could become so completely a stranger. Or perhaps he had been a stranger all along.

He felt her indifference, and let her go. Kindly, still not wanting to hurt him—for it was not his fault he was who he was; it was she who had changed, not he—she said, "Good night, Tom," and turned away, opening the building's thick glass door herself and walking through. After a long moment Tom descended the five granite steps to the silver limo waiting at the curb, and drove away.

In her apartment Catherine changed slowly into her nightgown and the black-and-peach flowered kimono her father had brought her from Hong Kong, washed her face and brushed the stiffness of spray out of her hair. It had been by all previous standards a lovely evening. She remembered a time when she would have welcomed Tom's careful manipulation of the conversation away from the unpleasant and the hurtful, and would have called it tact.

So why had it felt so dead?

Had she changed *that* much?

Not really, she thought, coming back into the bedroom, *if I've let Tom talk me into limping along with the shell of a relationship for the last eight months*. She knew in her heart that what was between them had ended when she'd walked out of the ballroom at the Barron. The assault, her disappearance, and all its consequences had been a side issue that Tom had used as an excuse, to himself and to her. And was still using, she supposed. A reason why it wasn't his fault.

A reason why her wishes in the situation were not as valid as his.

And, looking back at that beautiful debutante in her black dress and diamonds, limping to a stop on her high heels to wave at a cab, she wondered if she would have had the starch to break it off with Tom the following morning, had she reached home safely that night. Or would she simply have told herself, as she had so many times in the past, "Well, maybe I did overreact"?

She sighed, and shook her head at herself. Probably. There had been a time, when she'd just gotten out of the hospital, when she'd thought that her affection for Tom might well revive. These days Tom seemed to have forgotten that he had *never* been her one-and-only, however monogamous they had been sexually. Or had he simply assumed that in her flirtations with other men, her restless series of uneasy dates, she hadn't been looking for something different, something other than him?

Marriage, at one time a possibility—certainly what her father had hoped—now appeared only as a bizarre and horrifying vista of years of Tom's evasiveness, demands, and refusal to take her seriously.

She shook her head.

But in either case, it was over. Going out to nice restaurants, good theater, an evening of feeling beautiful and cherished, wasn't worth prolonging a relationship whose ashes were clearly dead and cold. *Not worth the aggro*, Edie would say, rolling those lovely bronze eyes and shrugging. And that, for Edie, would be that.

It was late, but the espresso at Alcazar had been strong and tomorrow was Sunday, and Catherine knew better than to go immediately to bed and spend the rest of the night arguing with Tom in a series of frustrating dreams. Instead she found her briefcase in its usual place beneath the secretaire, a delicate antique which these days doubled as a rather crowded office, since the apartment, for all its elegance, only had one bedroom. From it she fished a stack of court transcripts. The novel she was reading that week would be no match for Tom's intrusive presence in her mind, but there was nothing like a good legal wrangle that had to be sorted out by Monday to quash a mental conversation with someone who wasn't in the room.

She carried the transcripts into the bedroom, settled herself cross-legged on the silk of the comforter, and began to read.

(Public Defender: And what time did you see the defendant enter the Holiday Saloon on East 54th Street and say the words, 'I'm going to kill the sucker?'
Witness: About four-thirty in the afternoon.
Public Defender: And how long had you been in the Holiday Saloon at the time?
Witness: I dunno—since it opened.
Public Defender: And what time does the Holiday Saloon on East 54th Street open?
Witness: Six in the morning.)

Oh, swell, thought Catherine, *jury's gonna love that one.*

She stopped. Something froze inside her.

That had been a noise on the terrace.

Since the assault Catherine had never lost her awareness of anomalous noises, and Isaac's training had sharpened what had been mere nervousness into a cautious instinct for what was dangerous and what probably was not. Reaching over, she flicked off the bedside lamp; the French doors stood outlined in dark lattices against the glow thrown up by the city upon the clouds. She wasn't sure, but for a moment she thought she saw a shadow move.

The light in the living room was still on, and by its reflected glow she opened the bedside table and took out the .38 she had bought to keep in the apartment, shortly after starting to train in self-defense. On the range she was able to slaughter targets; in her heart she felt absolutely no doubt of her own willingness to kill a man if he came at her.

She wondered if the men who had slashed her had somehow learned she'd been to visit Carol Stabler. Carol had certainly been frightened of something.

Fire twice, she thought, repeating her range instructor's precepts as she slipped off the bed and glided silently toward the doors, the gun in both hands. *First one low, the kick'll throw your arm high for the head-shot.*

It had rained in the early hours of this morning, but by now the tiled terrace was dry. Just before the doors as she opened them she saw a packet wrapped in a flowered silk scarf. Old silk, faded and heavy, fringed 'thirties peau de soie.

A swift glance up and down the terrace showed her nothing but shadows. She bent, drew the scarf aside . . .

It was Vincent's old leather-bound copy of *Great Expectations*.

Her heart gave one hard slam and she stood up, gun in one hand, book and scarf in the other, and looked again.

And he was there, in the shadows of the plants at the end of the terrace, a hooded bulk of darkness from which shined the reflective eyes of a cat.

"Vincent!"

She saw the glint of his belt clasp as he stepped down from the little dais that held the plants, and the lights from the street below sheened faintly on leather and steel. "I didn't mean to frighten you," he began. "I'm sorry."

Three fast strides took her to him and she was in his arms before her mind completely registered the fact, the strength and warmth of his hold everything she had remembered, his voice nothing she would ever forget. "No," she breathed, her face half-buried in the soft roughness of his patched mantle, with its smells of candles and smoke. "No, I'm so glad to see you." *Glad* wasn't the word, any more than *pond* was the word to describe the depths of Crater Lake, but it would have to do.

His arms closed around her. Time stopped, and there was nothing but his presence.

After—*minutes*? she wondered, *eight months*?—he stepped back from her, looking down at her face in the barred reflection of the living room light. It was cold on the terrace, but not unbearably so, for the corner of the building and the screen of potted trees protected them, and the night was less bitter than the day had been.

"Your face . . ." Hesitant, he raised his hand to touch the smooth cheek but let it fall halfway.

She had forgotten he'd never seen her without

the cuts. "They fixed it," she said awkwardly. For a moment it flitted through her mind to wonder whether her mutilation had made her somehow less threatening to him, more accessible, but the thought only had to be formulated to be dismissed. Even had he not been what he was, Vincent was one of those people to whom physical beauty, though deeply appreciated for what it was, was entirely immaterial.

And with equal suddenness it clicked into place, from a thousand tiny remarks over the last few years, that Tom was not.

Vincent whispered, "Yes," still looking at her wonderingly. She took his hand.

"Come inside."

"No." He shook his head, drawing back from her. "I must go."

"No!" Her hand tightened on his. "Not . . . not yet."

He turned away, looking out into the city's jeweled darkness, and she heard the ragged draw of his breath. For a moment he was silent. When he spoke, there was passionate bitterness in his voice. "I shouldn't have come here."

"I'm glad you did." He looked back at her, a massive shape against the brilliant city, misery in every line and muscle of his shoulders and back. She set the book on the parapet—what she had done with gun and scarf she hadn't the faintest idea, though she found both later on the terrace near the doors—and sat on the edge of the plants' little dais in a corner out of the wind. "Come here," she said softly. "Sit down."

After a moment's hesitation during which she truly feared he would vanish into the night from which he had come—this time never to return—he came to her side. "I wanted to see you," he said softly. "There are things I wanted to tell you . . ."

"Me, too," she said, looking up into his face. "So many things."

"I know."

"It's been hard, Vincent . . ." She wondered, now, looking back on it, how she had ever managed to get through the last eight months alone.

"Yes." She heard the sorrow in his voice. He too had hurt.

She smiled a little. "I'm learning to be strong."

"I know." And looking into the jewel-colored eyes, she knew that he did. "Catherine, I feel the things you're feeling when *you* do."

Puzzled, she whispered, "How do you mean?"

"Just know it's true . . . and that your pain is my pain. Sometimes it's almost as if we're one."

That was something else, she thought, that she had sensed from the beginning, and hearing him say it did not surprise her. His hand moved toward hers, then drew back, as if he somehow feared the contact, or what the contact might mean.

After a moment he went on, "I came here because I wanted to see that you were well—and because I wanted to see you one last time."

The hurt of that, the shock, was like chill water in her veins. "I'll never see you again?"

He was silent a moment, thinking about that, head bowed so that his long mane hid his face. Then he said, "I've seen your world. There's no place for me in it." He looked up at her again, and his eyes gleamed in the shadows like molten gold. "I know what I am. Your world is filled with frightened people. And I remind them of what they're most afraid of."

"Their own ignorance," said Catherine softly, thinking of her initial reaction to the sight of that beautiful, alien face.

He shook his head. "Their aloneness."

Yes, she thought. Vincent was too *other* to be dealt with by those whose chief aim was to prove to themselves and everyone else that they came under the heading of *us* and not *them*. "Yes," she murmured.

"So now," he went on, "I have to begin to forget."

"Forget me?" It made sense to her, if he was ever to have any peace, any comfort again, but the thought was like watching the last companion on a very empty road walk away into the night, leaving her alone in darkness and cold.

"No," he said simply. "I'll never forget you. But I must forget the dream of being part of you." He stood, his heavy mantle whispering around him, and she saw his shoulders bowed, as if with the weight of the years to come. "Find someone to be part of, Catherine," he said. "Be happy." He turned away toward the parapet, toward whatever secret way down would take him back to his own world for good. "Good-bye."

"Wait . . ." She reached out, caught his sleeve. "Not yet. There's still time, it's still dark . . ."

He turned back, irresolute, and in his eyes she saw the pain of indecision, the pain of choice. He was, she knew, absolutely right, for him and for her. Friendship with her was impossible for him, perilous and, she understood now, filled with hurt; moreover her own feelings for him frightened her by their strength, and shook her to her bones.

What she should say, she knew, was *Good-bye*,

and, like him, learn to forget. But what she said was "Don't leave."

He stayed until almost dawn. It was far later than was safe; both knew it. But somehow there was always something else to say, or another chapter to read, sitting in the corner out of the wind, Vincent's mantle slung around both their shoulders against the cold. The black weight of the sky paled to charcoal, then suffused with pewter light as they read; and bathed in that wan opalescence, the bare trees of the park, the spiky cutouts of the buildings along Fifth Avenue, seemed to belong to another city entirely, one that Catherine had always known was there but had never quite seen.

"And as the morning mists had risen long ago when I first left the forge," she read to him, *"so the evening mists were rising now, and in all the broad expanse of tranquil light they showed me, I saw no shadow of another parting from her."*

Sixteen

SOMEBODY'S waiting for you," called one of the clerks as Catherine came through the office door.

She glanced automatically at the clock, half expecting it would show she was late and that whoever it was had been drumming their fingers for half an hour. But it was five till eight. *So much for a quiet day.*

The chaos in the D.A.'s office was no different from any other Monday morning: clerks threading their way through desks with stacks of files, memos, transcripts in hand; phones already ringing off the hook. A uniformed policeman had button-holed Joe Maxwell in a corner—poor Joe looked like he hadn't had his first coffee-transfusion of the day—and was explaining something at great length to him; Joe was nodding gravely. A big, courtly-looking Englishman whom Catherine vaguely recognized as one of the city's hundreds of private investigators was waiting with two more cops for Moreno to arrive at his office. All three looked like they'd been up all night.

But everything had changed.

She'd spent half of Sunday sleeping, the other

half walking quietly in the park, trying to sort through what she felt. What she felt, she knew, was unquestionably love, but a love with which she was entirely unfamiliar: a caring so powerful it hurt, and a peace that penetrated to the core of her soul. There was no sense of the restlessness or urgency she had known in her other affairs, no blood-fever of wondering what or how much he thought of her, or whether it would last. It seemed no more reasonable to wonder that than to wonder if she'd have her left hand next week.

He had come back to her. Against sense and reason, against every precept of her world and his, he had been there. And this morning all the world was new.

She came around the corner of a bank of filing cabinets to her cubicle and stopped, startled.

Carol Stabler was sitting beside her desk.

The younger woman looked haggard and nervous, perched on the hard plastic chair as if trying to make herself invisible and glancing worriedly around. Someone—probably Larry, a clerk who combined the efficiency of a machine gun with the motherly instincts of a hen with one chick—had given her a Styrofoam cup of coffee. She had drunk half of it, and was now engaged in picking bits off the rim.

Seeing her in good light for the first time—seeing all of her face—Catherine realized with a start that she had, in fact, seen her before. With a sense of watching the final pieces of a jigsaw puzzle fall into place she remembered Tom's party at the Barron—how endlessly long ago.

This girl had been there.

Catherine remembered her distinctly, as all details of that evening had replayed themselves over and over in her mind in the days of pain and darkness. She'd been wearing a red lamé dress that few other women would have had the style to carry off. She'd come down the wood-paneled curve of the ballroom stair during Catherine's argument with Tom.

She'd been very beautiful then. Even now, in spite of obvious damage to the facial nerves, she was still pretty, her fair, tousled-looking hair softly upswept, her green eyes and fresh skin carefully made up, big silver earrings complementing the delicate angle of the jaw. But her clothes looked old and a little shabby, the white sweater beginning to pill, the neat black trousers worn at the hem, as if the last eight months had been financially tight. And in repose her face had a weary, defeated look that changed to an expression of shaky determination when Catherine appeared in the doorway.

"Carol . . . I sure didn't expect to see you here."

"Yeah, well . . ." The girl's mouth flinched in a wry grimace. "I sure didn't expect to *be* here."

She pushed the coffee cup aside as Catherine took a seat at her desk, and sized her up, as if comparing, as Catherine had, the quick glimpse through a door crack into a darkened hall with the reality of what she saw. Perhaps, thought Catherine, Carol recognized her from the party as well.

In good light the resemblance between them was less striking, but then, she reflected, to some men all pretty little blondes looked alike.

Hesitantly, Carol went on, "I'm sorry about what they did to you. After you left that night I—I couldn't stop thinking about it." Her soft pink mouth tightened. "Maybe I can help you out."

A woman without much courage, thought

Catherine sympathetically, probably not even before she'd been beaten and mutilated. Anger at what had been done to her had not moved her to retaliate.

But as Catherine herself had found out, knowing that it had been done to another woman put it in a different light. They had passed within touching distance of each other that night. Carol's file had said the attack had taken place sometime between midnight and one in the morning. At a guess, Catherine's attackers had only realized they'd gotten the wrong woman when they'd gone through her purse in search of cash. They must have gone back to the Barron, either took her outside in the van or followed her home.

The thought of putting them behind bars was precisely like getting in a straight, hard counterpunch through Isaac's guard.

Gently, she asked, "Want to tell me what happened?"

Carol swallowed, started to reach for the half-dismembered coffee cup, then folded her hands again. Her nails, Catherine noticed, were painted a soft shell pink, well kept like the rest of her. She was a woman who had not lost her pride. When she spoke, her eyes met Catherine's squarely, without apology or pretense.

"I was working for this escort service," she said frankly. "It's called Mayfair; they had a pretty good clientele. You know . . . businessmen from out of town, that sort of thing."

Catherine knew. New York probably had more escort services than any city in the country, ranging from sleazeball dog-and-pony shows to the hire of well-groomed products of Eastern finishing schools who wouldn't disgrace a company president looking for a dinner companion at the Ritz. Of course, one of the planning commissioners, one of the big-time contractors, one of the investors, would have hired her for the evening.

It explained not only what Carol had been doing at Tom's party, but how the men had known to look for her there. No wonder the stocky hood's first question had been *Goin' home alone?*

Remembering that beautiful girl in the red dress, Catherine felt a spurt of bitter anger at the men who'd deadened the side of her face and left that fear-filled cringe in her eyes. She wondered if the woman were still working for a service, whose clients would be less particular about looks because they were paying $20 for a quick tumble in a rented room instead of $200 for a couple hours of dinner, drinks, and sophisticated pleasure.

Having seen the cheaper stables, for Carol's sake she hoped not.

But even a woman on the game never likes to be called a prostitute, so Catherine temporized: "You'd go out with them."

Carol nodded, and gave her a quick glance with wise green eyes. "Yeah, more or less. But Mayfair's run by this guy named Marty Belmont who's a real bad character." Now that she'd started talking, her words flowed easier, and her hands ceased their jittery quest for something to occupy them. Perhaps it was the calm of knowing that, for better or worse, she was in for the whole package. Perhaps it was only remembering a confidence she hadn't had since last April.

"Well," she sighed, "he started using the service to shake down the customers. Sometimes the girls would carry tape recorders . . ." Her mouth flexed

221

with dry distaste. "Sometimes Marty'd get it on film."

Catherine drew back, as if from a dirty smell. That too was not uncommon. In her months with the D.A.'s office she'd had half the dirty laundry of the city paraded under her nose. Though she didn't understand the particular quirk of the male nature that could compartmentalize a quick roll in the hay with a hired lady as something totally apart from the commitments of marriage, she knew such an attitude existed, and knew herself not qualified to judge the men who did it. But to record that momentary folly, to film it, to throw those secret needs back in the victim's face, disgusted her.

As when she and Edie had unearthed from the files the account of yet another Carol, aged sixty-three, being beaten up the same night they had by some other man, she could only figure dourly that she hadn't been in the D.A.'s office long enough. No wonder Joe Maxwell was an incurable cynic.

"How'd you get into trouble?"

Carol sighed, made a slight gesture with her hands. "I wouldn't go along with it," she said simply. "Belmont got it into his head that I was going to spill everything to the cops."

Yes, thought Catherine. Even a small show of integrity would scare a man like that.

"So he sent his men out for you . . . and me."

"So the men who attacked you, and me—they were Belmont's men?"

Carol shrugged. "Had to be."

The girl's fatalistic matter-of-factness awed her. She herself, behind her calm calculation of ways and means, felt again the flood of cool, deliberate rage. This young woman with her ruined face, she herself who would still be scraping together

222

pennies for plastic surgery if she hadn't happened
to have been—as everyone at Dad's office had
always said—Charles Chandler's daughter . . . they
had both been mutilated casually, almost off-
handedly, as a sidelight to some high-class hustler's
crummy scam. *One of those things*. Even her father,
hurt and enraged, had wanted the men caught
because they had done such a thing to his little girl.
Other men's little girls didn't enter into it, simply
because that was not how he thought.

Catherine wanted them because they had walked
away free.

"Will you testify against them with me?"

Carol hesitated for a long time. Then she said
softly, "Yeah. I'll testify."

Catherine had several other urgent projects due—
she always did, everyone in the office always did.
But with a little shuffling and a few phone calls she
pushed the three most pressing appointments back
till after noon, postponed a meeting with
Schumacher from Special Investigations, and
rounded up a mug book. Carol identified Marty
Belmont, a sleek, rather ferrety-looking man with
dark smooth hair and a mouth like a knife slit.

"The thing is," she said, looking up worriedly
and pushing back stray tendrils of flaxen hair from
her forehead, "I think he's still worried about me.
He phoned me once. Sometimes I think I've seen
his guys in my neighborhood."

Catherine remembered the chain on the door, the
scared voice inside. Whether Carol's fear was justi-
fied or not, like her own dread, just after her
release from the hospital, of every black van that
passed, scarcely mattered.

"Right now I'm just trying to get enough bread to split town."

She wondered again how Carol was making her living these days, but didn't ask. Whatever it was, it couldn't be paying much. Rent on anyplace in New York, even that shabby studio in Chelsea, would be eating up most of it, and more the longer she stayed to testify.

Carol also picked out the same photo Catherine had tentatively identified eight months ago as the stocky man in the bomber jacket who'd pushed her into the van.

"I don't know who he is," she said, turning the book around so Catherine could get a look at it. "But he's one of Belmont's."

"I thought he was," agreed Catherine. "I'd know his voice if I heard it, but it was so dark, and I only got a glimpse of him."

Carol sniffed ironically. "And he only got a glimpse of you."

After that it was easy. Another phone call set the wheels in motion for warrants: arrest and search of premises, to be served the following morning against Martin Belmont of the Mayfair Escort Service, 232 West 52nd, on the grounds of fraud, extortion, and aggravated assault . . . "for starters," Catherine finished, with a certain satisfaction. "I've got the affidavit of a witness."

Moreno was pleased. "We've had complaints about Mayfair Escort before," he said, when Catherine stopped briefly by his office on her way back to where Carol waited in the reception area. "But it was all anonymous, or so vague we couldn't get a handle on it. The men were scared to talk because they couldn't be sure when a packet of photographs might be showing up in their wife's mail—or their boss's.'' He shrugged his broad shoulders in their dark, striped wool, and chewed thoughtfully on a toothpick . . . he hadn't had a cigarette since just before she'd been hired. His desk was awash in papers, as it had been the day she'd arrived—every light on his phone was blazing like last month's Christmas tree.

''Chasing after these escort services is pretty low priority, you know,'' he went on. ''Personally, I could give a damn if every businessman who comes through town humps himself senseless. They're not hurting anybody, and God knows I've been in enough hotel rooms in strange towns to understand how they feel. But when it comes to blackmailing the customers, or hitting on the girls, that's when I get mad. You got your warrant for tomorrow morning, Chandler.''

It was long past noon—someone had gotten them sandwiches while Catherine was taking down the affidavit, but when Catherine returned to the waiting area she saw how the haunted, haggard look had returned to Carol's face. She looked up swiftly as Catherine came over.

''Okay,'' said Catherine briskly, ''we're all set. You're not going back to your apartment.'' She'd made a few phone calls for that, too.

Carol looked visibly relieved. ''Where am I going?''

''A friend of mine is renovating a brownstone in the Village.'' She fished from the pocket of her blue-gray jacket the slip of paper on which she'd written the address. ''There's not much in it, but it'll be a lot safer. Someone'll meet you with a key.''

What her old Radcliffe buddy Nell had said over the phone was ''Gee, you think someone might break in and steal some of the junk in that place? That'd save me a trip to the dump!" Good old Nell. Though Catherine wasn't as close to her as she was to Nancy or Jenny, Nell was the only friend she knew wealthy enough to possess something other than a miniscule New York apartment. *And if men can use the good-ol'-boys network,* she thought with grim amusement, *why not us 'Cliffies?*

"What about all my stuff?"

"We'll pick up your things tomorrow," Catherine assured her. "I'll bring whatever you need for tonight."

"Okay." She sounded uncertain—she'd had time to think about this again, and was getting scared.

Larry McKie appeared behind her, the slim, black clerk who'd greeted Catherine that morning with the news that someone was waiting for her. It seemed like days ago, now. Catherine nodded to him. "Larry'll give you a ride over. Call me as soon as you get there."

Carol nodded, and picked up her white fake-fur coat. She took a deep breath. "I guess there's no turning back, hunh?"

The two women regarded one another in silence for a moment, oddly alike: blonde and pretty, and intent upon the calm and legal enterprise of revenge for what had been done to them both. Catherine said, "Carol, you're sure you understand what the risks are? Don't do this for me. I don't want you to do anything that doesn't feel right."

Carol shook her head. The reflection of Catherine's strength gleamed in her soft green eyes. "I'm doing this for *me.*"

Catherine smiled and, stepping forward, embraced her quickly. "I'll see you tonight."

Larry, always well bred, helped Carol on with her coat, and Carol followed him out, jostling their way through the usual mob in the too-crowded bull pen toward the double doors that led to elevator, lobby, street.

Catherine watched them go, then slowly made her way back to her desk and the rest of the afternoon's impacted work. It had taken a lot of courage for Carol to come here, she knew, particularly if, as the girl had said, Marty Belmont had been more or less keeping tabs on her. He'd called her once, she'd said . . . Had that been all?

That was what had prompted Catherine to phone Nell and ask her to meet Carol and Larry there with the keys of the brownstone; the instinctive feeling that once Carol had taken the step of talking to the police, going back home would be a bad idea. She'd be safe enough there.

But Catherine still didn't like the idea that until the warrants were issued tomorrow morning, Marty Belmont and his men would still be walking around free.

Seventeen

I don't know what masochistic impulse ever prompted me to teach you to play chess." Father frowned through his square-lensed reading glasses at the board between them on the worn, time-stained wood of the octagonal table, trying to determine which of his bishops he could best afford to lose.

"Perhaps as a counterirritant to your rheumatism?" suggested Vincent soothingly. "Or a means of exercising the arteries by raising your blood pressure?" He watched impassively as Father moved one piece to safety, then, ignoring the other bishop, captured Father's queen with an unregarded knight.

"My arteries are in perfectly good condition," grumbled Father, and for a moment their eyes met over the board, Vincent's twinkling with solemn mischief. "Small thanks to you."

Faint echoes penetrated the room from the Long Chamber outside, where Sarah and Regan were preparing a communal supper for the workers who'd come back from the first successful tryout of Mouse's new pump. Through the doorway, around the curve of the rock-seam that communicated with this chamber, Vincent could see the uneven radiance of the kerosene lamps burning everywhere in that central square of the Tunnel community—the voices of children rose shrilly in a game of skatebroad-tag. The Tunnels were gradually returning to normal.

Father had taken the news of Vincent's visit to Catherine quietly. When he had said, as he had at the first, "Vincent, how could you?" there had been weary resignation rather than anger in his voice, as if he had feared all along that it would come to this.

"Father, how could I not?" Vincent had replied. "What was it Shakespeare said?

> *"Let me not to the marriage of true minds*
> *Admit impediments. Love is not love*
> *Which alters when it alteration finds . . .*
> *It is an ever-fixed mark . . .*
> *It is the star to every wandering bark . . ."*

Worsted with his own weapons, Father had only sighed. He had been, Vincent knew, very angry, but it had never occurred to Vincent not to tell him. Not only was their world too perilous, too fragile, to keep secret so great a potential risk—Vincent simply could not imagine lying, even by silence, to Father or to anyone else. Father's final comment had been, "I don't want you to be hurt—and I pray to God that if something goes wrong, hurt is all you'll be."

The old man looked haggard now, and very tired. He'd been working in the lower levels all day with the others, clearing mud and debris from communications passages and living chambers in

the wake of the retreating flood. According to
Mouse there were areas down there which would
remain innundated, and other tunnels which would
stay, half-blocked with mud or quicksand, for a
long time. But water was again moving to the
wellheads higher up, and the pressure-leaks in the
Old Main had mostly been repaired. Regan and her
children, William, Sarah, Bernardo and Zena, and
all the others were returning next week to their old
quarters on the lower levels. Ho's chamber they
had not troubled to clear.

Most of the girl's belongings had been destroyed.
But that was just as well, she had said, the last
time she'd spoken with Vincent in the cellar of a
Helper's apartment house in Harlem. There was
very little there that would have been of use to her,
above the ground.

Regarding Father now with guarded concern in
the wavering multiple shadows of the candles on
the table, seeing how gray his hair had grown, how
lined his face, Vincent reflected that there was a
certain amount to be said for Ho's opinion of what
the world Below could and could not give.

But for all the cold, and the damp that exacer-
bated the old injuries to Father's leg; for all its
eternal twilight and pitchy dark, it was safe. And
for Vincent, as for Father and so many of the
others—for Catherine too when she had needed it—
that quality of sanctuary was the critical thing.

"There," said Father, moving his knight. "Put
that in your pipe and smoke it."

Vincent tipped his head and studied the board,
quite rightly suspicious of the opening Father had
left his rook. It reminded him of a gambit in one
of Spassky's matches. If one reversed the positions
of the knight and the bishop's pawn it would be

exact. He reached out to block the danger with his queen's pawn . . .

And then he felt it, as if someone had struck him with a hammer in the chest.

Catherine?!?

Fear like the slice of a razor.

Fear and the certainty of death.

He was on his feet and out of the room before Father could draw breath to ask.

The brownstone Catherine's friend Nell had bought with her latest commission was just off Christopher, one of a streetful in the worst tangle of little mews and alleys around Sheridan Square. The overcast sky was darkening when Catherine's cab set her down in front of the place at four-thirty. She'd taken off work early to buy food, coffee, and a bottle of wine, with the intention of keeping Carol company and perhaps spending the night there herself if she could find something in the rooms full of mouse-nibbled junk that would double as a second bed.

Vincent had mentioned "Helpers," she recalled: people who gave the people of the Tunnels the old clothes they cut up and reconditioned, some of the food they ate, sometimes furniture, dishes, soap . . . whatever they could spare. She wondered, as she paid the driver and crossed the quiet pavement with her arms full of groceries, if she could somehow arrange for them to take what they needed from the rooms full of junk that had been there, in Jenny's phrase, since God left for Detroit. Nell had been trying for months to line up a truck, a free day, and a big enough crew of friends to haul it all down to the city dump, and hadn't succeeded yet. She'd have to speak to Vincent, the next time she saw him, and to Nell, about setting that up.

It occurred to her that she was on her way to becoming a Helper herself.

The thought brought Vincent back to mind, and she smiled. At one point Saturday night she had asked him how he had known she had courage and strength, at a time when she hadn't known it herself. He had ducked his head a little, half smiling. "When you first saw me in the reflector," he had said, and she'd blushed with shame at the memory of her own horror. "Your first instinct was not to run or hide . . . it was to throw something at me as hard as you could. And so I knew." And she had laughed, leaning her cheek on the strength of his shoulder.

The front steps were tall, giving the house, like all those on the street, a snooty air which reminded her of her formidable Grandmother Heathcott. In cement urns dead plants flanked the door, with its tarnished hardware and old-fashioned brass finger-plate. Twisting the antique bell-switch, Catherine heard a muffled chime speak out somewhere in the lofty hall. But no footsteps came treading down the stairs within.

She glanced up and down the street in the misty gray gloom. It was possible Carol had walked down to the corner store for cigarettes—in this neighborhood it should be a pretty safe thing to do. Only—did Carol smoke? Nervous as she'd been in the office she hadn't lit up.

Catherine frowned a little to herself as she dug into her trouser pocket for the duplicate key Nell had sent back to her via Larry; and let herself in.

"Carol?"

Her voice echoed up the boxy corners of the

paneled stairwell that rose from the hall. Down here was a well of ash-colored shadow. The paneling—miles of it—had been stripped and partially refinished, though the discolored plaster of the walls had not yet been painted. Most of Nell's friends, Jenny and Catherine included, worked schedules far too hectic to permit more than an occasional weekend or evening per month at the task. Just under the stairs a shut door led, Catherine knew, to the cellar, and beyond that a hall stretched, a weird and gloomy maze of shut doors, like a house in a frightening dream. Traffic noises from Sheridan Square sounded loud in the stillness. Rush hour was well under way. Looking up the stairs, Catherine could see on the third floor the bluish reflection of a television's light, and hear its muffled staccato murmur.

Fallen asleep in front of it? she wondered, and then remembered Carol's extreme nervousness—the slightest sound would have had her awake. More likely she'd left it on when she went out. A lot of people did.

But something about the dusk-filled house prickled at Catherine's nerves. She set the bag of groceries down on the bottom step, and ascended cautiously, quietly, listening for anomalous sound.

Carol was in the bedroom, where the TV set flickered with some tale of well-dressed adultery and addiction in stylish settings.

She was quite dead.

Catherine knew it even as she hurried forward and knelt beside the sprawled body on the stained and grimy Axminster. She felt a sickening stab of guilt—she'd thought of getting Carol away from her apartment, but never that Belmont would have had the girl followed.

She turned her over. The blonde hair fell aside from the face, showing it swollen and purple. The green eyes stared up at her, the tongue protruded slightly from between puffed lips. She'd been strangled. The finger weals were red on her throat beneath the white collar of her sweater.

Obliquely, Catherine was glad she'd gone to the morgue in the course of several investigations that summer—at least the mere sight of a dead human being didn't give her the shakes anymore. Some of Isaac's more gruesome methods of training had helped with that too.

But the bodies in the morgue hadn't been anyone she'd known. They hadn't been a woman she'd hugged good-bye three hours previously.

The body wasn't even cold.

She felt for a pulse, knowing it wouldn't be there, and it wasn't. But she had to try.

"Don't bother," said a voice behind her, the same voice she remembered from a hundred nightmares over the last eight months . . . *Goin' home alone, Carol?*

Catherine swung around, her heart lurching into her throat and a slam of sheer adrenaline and fear slicing through her.

(*Catherine?!?*)

The stocky man who'd pushed her into the van stood framed in the doorway, still in the light-gray bomber jacket that was the only garment she'd remembered. Beside him was a man she recognized from the mug shots as Marty Belmont.

"She's dead," said the stocky man. He held up his hand, and like magic a switchblade flipped into it, the cold leaf of steel flashing in the phosphoric TV-light.

Belmont added, "And so are you."

They advanced on her.

They advanced together, and Catherine's reaction, hammered into her by Isaac in endless drills on the stained old tatamis, was automatic and instinctive. Even as she grabbed the base of the pole lamp beside the TV she thought fleetingly that if they'd had any brains they would have split and come at her from two sides. The six-foot brass pole, cord trailing, was long enough to smash across both their chests, knocking them backwards with all the driving force of her spring. The stocky guy, dumped on his ample keester, made a futile grab at her as she did a diving end-run around him and out the door.

Belmont was yelling something behind her as Catherine plunged down the stairs. Feet thundered at the bottom; looking over the rail she saw dim light from above falling on a hairy arm tattooed with a dragon, another shadow racing up behind, the driver of the van, probably. She wheeled and darted back up the stairs and into the inky pit of the second-floor hall, with its nightmare maze of doors.

The back of the house would be safer than the front, she thought. They'd check doors as they came to them, it would give her a chance to find a weapon. In spite of their handiness as makeshift ice picks, she'd given up wearing spike heels, and in any case even Fetish Specials wouldn't lessen the odds against a knife. A knife might not be all they had, either. The room she ducked into had been a bedroom, doors leading from it into other bedrooms, bathrooms, dressing rooms, all choked with the dirty masses of furniture Nell had complained so loudly about all fall: rump-sprung easy chairs, gutted sofas, rotting cardboard boxes filled with newspapers, old bottles, magazines.

Picture frame? No—too light, they could punch through it or knock it aside and it didn't give her enough distance. A chair was what she needed . . . a wood kitchen chair, not the overstuffed jobs that seemed to be wadded into every corner.

Calling out—screaming—was out of the question. This was New York, and any sound would bring Belmont and Company down on her a lot faster than it would bring help.

She wondered if Carol had screamed.

She crouched still, listening. Out in the hall she could hear voices and the banging of doors, like one of those ridiculous French farces . . . open one door, close another, open two doors and run in and out. Her heart was beating hard with fear. "Where'd she go?" "Try in there." "She's gotta be in one of these."

Directly to her right the door jerked open and inwards, blocking her from the view of whoever looked inside. It closed again with a slam. *French farce time for sure.* If they gave up, thought she'd gone . . .

"She's here someplace."

They weren't buying it; they'd hunt till they found her. She glanced across the room at the window—painted shut since 1936, according to Nell. It would take a crowbar to raise the sash. She might succeed in breaking it, but she also might succeed in breaking her leg jumping down. Still . . .

She caught up a spindly-legged wooden stool, crossed the room softly, taking her weight on her toes so the tapping of her heels wouldn't alert them. The window looked onto the alley in the back. As far as she could see by angling her head there was a sunken areaway below, adding another half-story to her drop and the chance of killing herself on steel railings and whatever else might be down there.

Footsteps thudded in the hall. She stepped back, looking for cover, and her heel caught the edge of one of those infernal cardboard boxes of junk. This one contained old perfume-bottles, and they went over with the crash of doom.

The door slammed open as Catherine took one long stride toward it and smashed the stool with all her strength into the men as they came through. It was the stocky hood and the man with the tattoo. Taken by surprise, they stumbled back, and, doubling like a hare, Catherine plunged through another door, into an old dressing room and the bedroom beyond and out again into the hall, heading for the stair. She'd left the door at the bottom unlocked. If she could just make it that far . . .

Another man she didn't recognize—probably the driver of the van—blocked her way, but by this time Catherine was past caring. As he grabbed her she kneed him full-force in the groin, slammed an elbow across his face, and scrambled over him as he went down cursing. He grabbed at her ankles and she fell hard on the wooden flights, bruising hands and arms, barely feeling it as she lunged down, trying to kick off the terrifying grip on her ankles.

She couldn't—he had her, holding her, dragging her back. She twisted and grabbed for the neck of the wine bottle sticking out of the grocery bag on the bottom step. The cold glass slipped from her fingertips; she lunged again, dragging against the terrifying strength of him, and seized the makeshift weapon.

"Hold it." Belmont stood at the top of the flight. He had a gun. Catherine knew she'd lost.

He came down quietly, gun trained on her. Behind him the tattooed punk was nursing a surprising array of lacerations and bruises where the stool's legs had caught him, the stocky man in the bomber jacket flipping his switchblade behind. Panting, burning with adrenaline and fear, Catherine lay on the steps and watched them approach, waiting, gauging her distance for a final strike if she could manage it and knowing there was no way she could.

Belmont stooped before her, pointed the gun down at her head. He smiled. "Say good night," he said.

And deep in the bowels of the house came another sound, a rending crash, the clatter of bricks falling, and something—cry—roar—an elemental bellow of desperation, savagery, and animal rage.

Belmont gasped "What the—" and was in the act of rising when the oak door to the cellar stairs exploded from within like shattering balsa, and something huge and tawny and terrible burst from the underground darkness and fell upon him like the God of Death.

Belmont screamed once, as the gun and most of the flesh were ripped from his hand. Catherine, staring up in numbed shock, saw Vincent swat the man aside with the hellish speed of a cat killing a roach. Bellowing like a lion-demon, fangs flashing in the dim glow of the street lamps outside, Vincent swung around as the stocky man made a swipe at him with the switchblade; his clawed hand struck the man's face, then his chest, his throat.

Feral, deadly, he seemed to swirl in a tawny cloud of rage, and as if the tattooed punk and the driver knew that he would never let them escape they lunged at him, this unknown beast with his dark mantle and blazing eyes. His strength was terrifying and his speed more so—like an animal he fought full-bore, without hesitation or timing or thought, only from instinct and killing rage. Catherine, flattened to the newel-post at the bottom of the stairs, was never in doubt of the outcome; the punk was picked up like a rag doll and flung aside with a broken neck, the driver, turning at last to flee, dragged down and mauled before he had gone two strides.

It was over almost before it had begun.

Catherine's breath leaked slowly from her lips— she realized she'd drawn it in, that first second when Vincent had crashed through the splinters of the cellar door, and had not let it out . . .

Vincent slumped back from the body of the driver. There was blood on his claws, his mantle . . . tipping the ends of his honey-colored mane and spattering the bare plaster of the walls. He bowed his head, and in the broken square of yellowish light from the window Catherine saw his face—the face of a beast, contorted with the awareness of a man who understands what he has done.

But the feral rage in him had been her own, the afternoon she'd broken through her own fear and gone after Isaac in the loft—and today, when she'd fought for her own life.

And if Vincent was other than human, what did that make Belmont and his men?

Distantly, sirens had begun to sound.

Catherine scrambled hurriedly to her feet. Her

knees were shaking as she stepped over the fallen bodies, her hands, when she reached down to grasp Vincent's bloodied fingers, trembled with shock. He looked up quickly at her touch, and for an instant she saw in his eyes shame and uncertainty, as if wondering how she could come near him after seeing his other, dark, unhuman side.

And for an instant their gazes locked, and he saw in her eyes his own reflection, her understanding of the darkness because a part of it was her own.

They were, Catherine understood, yang and yin; but which of them was the fire, and which the night, she could not tell.

"We can't stay here," she whispered, and drew him to his feet, as he had once drawn her.

A hole had been kicked and ripped in the wall of the basement, the bricks literally clawed out from within. Through a ragged slit of shattered plaster and broken foundation the curved sides of an old cement main could be seen, vanishing away into the inky shadows of the night below the ground. The tough flesh of Vincent's hands, Catherine saw now, was ripped and abraded, his dark mantle torn and streaked with plaster dust and mud.

He had done this, she thought. He had done this when he'd felt her fear.

She took his hand; together they stepped into the darkness.

The local section of the following morning's *Times* briefly reported the deaths of Martin Belmont and three others in the basement of a Greenwich Village townhouse belonging to Ms. Elinor Fletcher, with a brevity which implied that the four were scarcely a loss to the community at large. It also mentioned that the body of one Carol Stabler had been found upstairs, but on the whole, between them District Attorney Moreno and Joe Maxwell managed to keep the lid on the whole affair. It is possible that a number of men in the Tri-State area—and several women as well—breathed easier as they went about their business that day.

The article made mention in passing of a hole in the cellar wall leading into an old steam tunnel that was found to be firmly closed off with an iron safety-gate thirty feet down its length; there was no report that anyone had tried to force the gate or see what lay beyond it.

Ms. Stabler, the article said, a witness in protective custody, had been strangled. The four men, in spite of the patent unlikeliness of such a thing happening in downtown New York, appeared to have been mauled to death by a lion.

"I owe you . . . everything," said Catherine quietly.

Vincent shook his head. "You owe me nothing."

They had come to the first of the great chasms that guarded the inner levels, spanned by its three arched, ancient bridges. Jury-rigged lamps, burning feebly along one wall, filled the vast space with a mysterious, smoke-colored twilight, and the huge cavern echoed softly with the tapping of the pipes, the heartbeat of the world Below. Behind her, Catherine knew the long, winding metal stair ascended to the drainage-tunnel in Central Park. It would be a very short walk back to her home.

"I'm part of you, Catherine," he said, "just as you're a part of me. Wherever you go, wherever I am—I'm with you."

She stood for a moment, gazing up at him in the sulfurous dusk. *I'm with you . . .*

She stepped forward into his arms.

How long they stood together Catherine didn't know. Like their first embrace upon the terrace, it might have lasted a minute or eight months, or all of their lives. It was good to feel the warm, breathing presence of him, the muscles of his shoulder beneath the shabby robes he wore, the strength of his arm, and of his spirit.

She had no idea where this would end, no idea where it might lead her. She only knew that they were bound together, she and this strange and beautiful soul, and the thought, rather than uncertainty, brought her peace.

Vincent stepped back from her, the rough-textured beauty of his voice echoing softly in the gloom, moving already toward the narrow span of bricks that bridged the abyss between her world and his. "Good-bye . . ." he said.

Catherine paused, turning from the stair that led up toward the light. "For now," she said, and added Estella's final line to Pip from the end of *Great Expectations:* "'*And will continue friends apart.*'"

For a moment he turned back, and in the shadows of his mane, she saw his blue eyes smile.

The Timeless Romances
of New York Times Bestselling Author

JOHANNA LINDSEY

TENDER REBEL   75086-4/$4.50 US/$5.95 Can
Insisting on a marriage in name only was something Roslyn quickly grew to regret as she dared to trust her new husband with her life...and her love.

SECRET FIRE   75087-2/$4.50 US/$5.95 Can
From the tempestuous passion at their first meeting, theirs was a fever that carried them to the power of undeniable love.

HEARTS AFLAME   89982-5/$3.95 US/$5.75 Can
Enemies in an age of war, they were lovers in passion's timeless battle.

A HEART SO WILD   75084-8/$4.50 US/$5.95 Can
Searching for her father in Indian territory, Courtney put her faith in Chandos—little dreaming of the dark secret that burned in his soul or the fires that he would ignite in her.

WHEN LOVE AWAITS	89739-3/$3.95 US/$5.50 Can
LOVE ONLY ONCE	89953-1/$4.50 US/$5.50 Can
TENDER IS THE STORM	89693-1/$3.95 US/$5.50 Can
BRAVE THE WILD WIND	89284-7/$3.95 US/$5.50 Can
A GENTLE FEUDING	87155-6/$4.50 US/$5.50 Can
HEART OF THUNDER	85118-0/$3.95 US/$4.75 Can
SO SPEAKS THE HEART	81471-4/$3.95 US/$4.75 Can
GLORIOUS ANGEL	84947-X/$3.95 US/$4.95 Can
PARADISE WILD	77651-0/$3.95 US/$5.50 Can
FIRES OF WINTER	75747-8/$4.50 US/$5.50 Can
A PIRATE'S LOVE	40048-0/$3.95 US/$4.95 Can
CAPTIVE BRIDE	01697-4/$3.95 US/$4.95 Can

AVON BOOKS

Buy these books at your local bookstore or use this coupon for ordering:

Avon Books, Dept BP, Box 767, Rte 2, Dresden, TN 38225
Please send me the book(s) I have checked above. I am enclosing $_____
(please add $1.00 to cover postage and handling for each book ordered to a maximum of three dollars). *Send check or money order*—no cash or C.O.D.'s please. Prices and numbers are subject to change without notice. Please allow six to eight weeks for delivery.

Name _____

Address _____

City _____ State/Zip _____

Lindsey 12/88

KAREN ROBARDS

**THE MISTRESS OF ROMANTIC MAGIC
WEAVES HER BESTSELLING SPELL
AGAIN AND AGAIN...**

TIGER'S EYE
75555-6//$3.95 US/$4.95 Can
Theirs was a passion that could
only be called madness—but
destiny called it love!

DESIRE IN THE SUN
75554-8/$3.95 US/$4.95 Can
Love wild, love free—dangerous,
irresistible, inexpressibly sweet!

DARK OF THE MOON
75437-1/$3.95 US/$4.95 Can
The sweeping tale of a daring woman,
a rebellious lord, and the flames
of their undeniable love.